ANIMAL FACTS

Anita Ganeri

D0027161

CONTENTS

Illustrated by Tony Gibson and Ian Jackson

**Additional illustrations by
Pam Corfield**

**Designed by Tony Gibson
and Steve Page**

**Consultant: Michael Boorer,
Education Officer, London Zoo**

What is a mammal?

How many mammals?

There are over 4,000 different kinds of mammals in the world. These are divided into 19 groups called 'orders'. The rodent order is the biggest with about 1,750 species, while the aardvark is the only living member of its order. There are very few mammals in the world compared to other animals and there are hundreds of times more insects than there are mammals.

DID YOU KNOW?

All mammals breathe air. The distant ancestors of mammals were fish and mammals still have some traces of gills for breathing underwater. The tube running between a mammal's ear and its throat is really a gill-slit.

Central heating

Mammals are warm-blooded. This means that the temperature inside their bodies stays about the same whatever the weather is like outside. Most mammals have a body temperature of about 36°C-39°C (97°F-102°F).

Warm blood allows mammals to be very active and to live in a wide variety of places, from the icy Poles to the hot Tropics. Fur and fat help protect them from the cold and they get rid of excess heat by sweating or panting.

Hair history

Mammals are the only animals with true hair. Hairs are dead cords of a substance called keratin which is also found in nails. What looks like hair on spiders and flies actually contains living parts of the animal. All mammals have some hair, though you would need a magnifying glass to see the fine hair on the lips of a young whale.

Backbones

Mammals are vertebrates which means that they all have backbones. Most of the animals in the world have no backbone. All mammals, except for some sea-cows and sloths, have seven bones in their necks. This includes giraffes whose necks can be 2 m (6½ ft) long and mice who seem to have no neck at all.

The kinds of living mammals

Family	Examples	Number of species
Rodents	Rats, mice, squirrels, porcupines	about 1,750
Chiropterans	Bats	about 950
Insectivores (insect eaters)	Shrews, hedgehogs	300
Carnivores (meat eaters)	Dogs, cats, bears, weasels	about 250
Marsupials (pouched mammals)	Kangaroos, possums	about 240
Primates	Bush babies, monkeys, apes	about 180
Ungulates (even-toed)	Cattle, deer, hippos, pigs	about 180
Cetaceans	Whales and dolphins	about 85
Lagomorphs	Rabbits and hares	about 60
Pinnipedes	Seals, sealions, walruses	32
Edentates	Armadillos, sloths, giant anteaters	about 30
Ungulates (odd-toed)	Tapirs, rhinos, horses	15
Pangolins	Scaly anteaters	7
Monotremes (egg layers)	Platypus, spiny anteaters	6
Hyraxes		6
Sirenians	Sea cows and manatees	4
Dermopterans	Flying lemurs	2
Elephants		2
Aardvark		1

Care for the young

All mammals look after their young and feed them on milk. They are the only animals that produce milk. The length of time a baby is looked after by its parents varies from a few weeks for mice to several years for apes.

Earflaps

Mammals are the only animals with flaps around their ears. These direct sound down into the ears. Some sea and burrowing mammals have lost their earflaps as they have become adapted for life in the water or underground.

Poison

Only two types of mammal are poisonous. Some shrews have a slightly poisonous bite. Male platypuses have poisonous spurs on their back legs.

3

The first mammals

Reptile relations

About 250 million years ago most land animals were reptiles. About 200 million years ago some began to develop into mammals. One of the earliest mammals, Megazostrodon, lived 190 million years ago in Africa. It was about 10 cm (4 in) long and looked like a shrew.

Mammals on the move

At the time when the dinosaurs died out, 65 million years ago, mammals began to develop more fully into the three main groups we have today:

Monotremes are those mammals which lay eggs such as the duck-billed platypus.

Marsupials are mammals with pouches. They give birth to tiny babies which crawl into the mother's pouch to feed on milk until they are fully developed.

Placental mammals are the largest group. The baby grows and is nourished inside the mother's body until it is born.

Prehistoric pouches

Millions of years ago, two kinds of giant marsupials lived in Australia. Procoptodon was a huge kangaroo, about 3 m (10 ft) tall, twice the height of a modern kangaroo. Diprotodon was a giant wombat and the largest marsupial ever. It weighed as much as a hippopotamus.

Horse race

The first horses lived about 55 million years ago in the North American forests. Hyracotherium was only the size of a fox and had toes on its feet. Horses grew bigger and developed hooves so they could run faster. Equus, the modern horse, first lived about 2 million years ago.

DID YOU KNOW?

Paraceratherium was the biggest land mammal there has ever been. It lived about 35 million years ago in Asia and Europe and was 8 m (26 ft) tall and 11 m (36 ft) long. It looked like a gigantic rhinoceros but had a long neck like a giraffe. Six people, walking side by side, could easily have passed underneath it.

Super sloth

Megatherium was a type of giant sloth which lived about 15,000 years ago. It was as high as a modern elephant and over 6 m (19 ft) in length. Today's sloths are about a tenth of its size.

First diets

Most early mammals ate insects and worms. Carnivores or meat-eaters first lived about 35 million years ago. The largest carnivore ever lived 20 million years ago. Megistotherium was bigger than a grizzly bear. It attacked and killed huge elephants. One of the fiercest carnivores was Smilodon, the sabre-toothed tiger. It had long pointed teeth for tearing meat apart.

The first elephants lived 40 million years ago. Moeritherium was only as big as a large pig and had no tusks or trunk. Today's African elephant is 300 times bigger. Deinotherium, which lived 15 million years ago, was much larger than today's elephants. It had tusks which curved back towards its chest. It probably used them like forks to dig up food.

Thunder beast

The giant mammal, Brontotherium, or 'thunder beast', lived 35 million years ago in North America. It was about the size of a hippo and had a forked horn on the end of its nose, perhaps for fending off enemies. This huge creature ate only leaves and fruit.

Little and large

The ancestors of today's camels lived about 10 million years ago. Unlike modern camels, they had no humps. Stenomylus was a tiny animal, only as big as a small deer. Alticamelus was about 3 m (10 ft) tall, with long legs and a long neck, like a giraffe's, for reaching leaves high up in the trees.

Sea giant

A giant whale, Basilosaurus, was the largest prehistoric sea mammal. It was more than 20 m (65 ft) long, about 7 m (13 ft) smaller than a blue whale, the largest sea mammal alive today. It lived 40 million years ago.

Baby mammals

Tail first

The biggest animal baby is a blue whale calf. Unlike most mammals, whales and dolphins are born tail first. Because it is born underwater, the baby has to be pushed quickly to the surface by its mother so that it can breathe. A new-born calf can only stay underwater for about 30 seconds at a time.

Marsupial mother

When a baby kangaroo, or 'joey', is born it is only about the size of a bee and is blind and helpless. The joey crawls into its mother's pouch and stays there for six months, feeding on milk and growing. It comes out of the pouch for the first time after about 28 weeks and leaves the pouch for good after about 33 weeks.

DID YOU KNOW?

All the pet hamsters in the world are descended from the same mother. This was a female wild hamster found with a litter of 12 babies in 1930 in Syria.

Smallest babies

The smallest mammal babies are probably those of the mouse opossums in Central and South America. The new-born babies of some species are only as big as grains of rice.

Egg layer

When the duck-billed platypus was discovered in 1797 people thought that it must be either a duck or a reptile because it was found to lay eggs. The female builds her nest in a river bank tunnel and in it lays soft, sticky eggs. But when the babies hatch they feed on their mother's milk showing that the platypus is in fact a mammal, although a very strange one.

Who am I?

An elephant in the Kruger National Park South Africa chose its own family and now thinks it is a buffalo. It was brought to the park in the 1970s with four other elephants to live near a herd of buffalo.

This elephant soon joined the herd and was accepted as being part of it. It was seen by park rangers drinking from a waterhole with its new buffalo 'family' and running off when a herd of elephants came near.

Mammals and their babies

Mammal	Average pregnancy	Usual number of young
Asian elephant	20 months	1
Indian rhinoceros	18 months	1
Giraffe	15 months	1
Blue whale	11 months	1
Human being	9 months	1
Chimpanzee	8 months	1
Dog	2 months	3-6
Red kangaroo	35 days	1
House mouse	19 days	4-32
American opossum	13 days	10

Most babies

The mammal which has the most young is the common vole. It can have its first litter when it is only 15 days old and has 4-9 babies as often as 15 times a year. In her lifetime, a female vole may have 33 litters, a total of as many as 147 young.

Growing up fast

The striped tenrec in Madagascar is the mammal which grows up the fastest. Two babies born in Berlin Zoo in July 1961 could run almost at once and eat worms by the age of six days. Other mammals can still only drink their mother's milk at this age.

Longest pregnancy

The mammal which has the longest pregnancy (called the gestation period) is an Asian elephant. The pregnancy lasts for 20-22 months, 33 times as long as that of a house mouse. Another female elephant from the herd who is called the 'auntie' helps look after the new baby.

Shortest pregnancy

An American opossum has a pregnancy of only 12-14 days and it may even be as short as eight days. The babies, though, still need to spend another 10 weeks feeding in their mother's pouch before they are fully developed.

Amazing But True

The nine-banded armadillo gives birth to sets of identical quads. Most mammals have babies which look different and are of different sexes. Armadillo quads are always identical and always of the same sex.

Mammal lives

Grand old age

The mammal which lives the longest, after man, is the Asian elephant. The oldest on record was called Modoc. She died in California, USA in July 1975, at the age of 75. During her long career in the circus, Modoc survived two attempts to poison her and a terrible fire. The fire made her a heroine when she dragged the lions' cage out of the big top tent to safety. She starred in several TV series before retiring.

Sea life

Baird's beaked whale is the longest–living sea mammal known. It can live for up to a maximum of about 70 years.

Oldest horse

The oldest known horse was born in 1760 and died at the age of 62 in Lancashire, Britain. He spent most of his long life towing barges along the canals before he was retired to a farm in 1819. Horses are usually expected to live for about 25-30 years.

Ancient Nero

Nero, a lion in the Cologne Zoo, West Germany, died at the age of 29 in May 1907. This made him the longest-lived big cat. In the wild lions grow more slowly than in zoos. They usually live for 12-14 years and rarely for 20 years. The oldest tiger was an Indian tigress in the Adelaide Zoo, Australia who lived for 26 years and 3 months.

Life on the wing

Bats normally live for 10-20 years. The oldest bat known is an Indian flying fox. It died at London Zoo at the age of 31 years and 5 months.

Amazing But True

Lemmings are small, hamster-like rodents from Norway. Their lives seem to go in strange four year cycles. For the first three years the lemmings breed at an ever-increasing rate. Then they seem to panic at the overcrowding and leave their homes in millions to find more space. Their mad rush carries them until they reach rivers or the sea. Even then they plunge in and try to swim across but most drown.

Mammal life-spans

Human being	60-80 years
Asian elephant	70-75 years
Killer whale	50-70 years
Rhinoceros	20-50 years
Hippopotamus	40-50 years
Arabian camel	25-40 years
Chimpanzee	30-40 years
Bottle-nosed dolphin	25-40 years
Zebra	20-30 years
Red deer	Up to 20 years
Giraffe	15-25 years
Koala	15-20 years
Grey kangaroo	15-20 years
Giant anteater	Up to 14 years
Two-toed sloth	8-12 years
European hedgehog	6 years
European rabbit	Up to 5 years
Armadillo	4 years
Rat	4 years
Mole	3-4 years
Long-tailed shrew	12-18 months

Cats and dogs

Domestic cats usually live longer than dogs. The oldest cat was probably a tabby called Puss in Devon, Britain. She died in November 1937, one day after her 36th birthday. The oldest dog was an Australian cattle dog called Bluey who lived for 29 years and 5 months. Dogs usually live for about 8-15 years.

Shortest life

The tiny shrew has the shortest life-span of all the mammals. Most shrews live for only about 12-18 months in the wild. They are born one year, breed the next year and then die. The record life-span for a shrew in captivity is 2 years and 3 months.

What mammals eat

Regular meals

Because they are warm-blooded, mammals can be very active in both hot and cold weather. They need a lot of energy for hunting, finding homes and looking after their young. They get their energy from food and must eat regularly.

No drink

Koalas will only eat the leaves of five out of the 350 kinds of eucalyptus tree. The word 'koala' means 'no drink' in the Aborigine language and koalas almost never need to drink water, getting all the liquid they need from the leaves they eat.

Giant anteater

The South American giant anteater has a 60 cm (24 in) long tongue which it uses to catch ants – its staple diet. It tears open an anthill with its strong claws and pokes its sticky tongue around inside until it is coated with ants, then flicks it out and swallows the ants whole. It can do this twice a second and can easily catch well over 30,000 ants a day.

Liquid diet

Vampire bats live on a diet of animal blood. They hunt at night and attack animals while they are asleep. The bat's saliva contains a substance which stops the blood from clotting and closing the wound. A great vampire bat weighs about 28 g (1 oz) and drinks about a tablespoonful of blood a day.

Excuse fingers

The aye-aye, a rare lemur in Madagascar, has long, thin middle fingers. It eats wood-boring insects. To catch them, the aye-aye knocks on the tree bark, listens for the insects to move, pokes its skewer-like finger inside and pulls them out.

Mammal diets		
Mammal	**Food**	
Rhinoceros	plants, leaves, grass	
Fruit-bat	fruit, flowers, nectar	
Gorilla	leaves, plants	
Polar bear	seals, fish	
Cheetah	antelopes, gazelles	
Hedgehog	insects, worms	
Tarsier	birds, lizards, insects	
Long-tailed macaque	crabs, shell fish, fruit	
Panda	bamboo, rats, snakes, flowers	

Herbivore (plants)	**Carnivore** (meat)	**Omnivore** (both)

High table

A giraffe's long neck allows it to reach its favourite food of leaves on branches up to 6 m (20 ft) off the ground. It uses its 40 cm (16 in) long tongue to grip and pull branches down so it can strip off the leaves with its rubbery lips.

Giant hunger

In spring and summer, a blue whale eats as much as four tonnes of food a day, about twice as much as a well-fed person eats in a year. It swims, mouth wide open, through the sea, sucking in thousands of litres of water which contains krill (tiny shrimp-like creatures). Instead of teeth, the whale has huge bony plates called baleen hanging down inside its mouth. They strain the water, leaving the krill.

DID YOU KNOW?

Elephants eat up to ½ tonne of plant food a day. They have 24 teeth for grinding it. The teeth do not grow all at once, but in fours. As the first set wears down, a second set grows. At the age of 45 an elephant grows its last teeth, each weighing 4 kg (9 lb).

Eyes, ears and noses

Super smell

Dogs have an excellent sense of smell. An Alsatian has 44 times more smell cells in its nose than a human being. It can smell things about one million times better than man. Dogs also have superb hearing. They can pick up much higher sounds than human ears are able to hear.

DID YOU KNOW?

In 1925 Sauer, a Dobermann Pinscher, tracked two thieves 160 km (100 miles) across the Great Karroo desert in South Africa just by following their scent.

Wide-eyed

The biggest mammal in the world, the blue whale, has the biggest eyes. They are as big as footballs, quite small for its huge size but over six times wider than a human eye and 150 times wider than a pygmy shrew's eyes.

What big eyes . . .

Animals that feed at night have special ways of finding their way in the dark. Some, such as moles and bats, have tiny eyes but very good hearing and smell. Others, such as bush babies and tarsiers, have huge-fronted eyes. The Eastern tarsier's eyes are 17 mm (0.6 in) across. If a human's eyes were the same size in proportion to its body, they would be as big as grapefruit.

Big ears

An African elephant has huge earflaps. Each is about 1.8 m (6 ft) across and nearly as big as a single bed sheet. Elephants flap their ears to keep cool and a female beats her ears on her back to call her young. An elephant spreads out its ears to make it look more threatening to enemies.

Ear conditioning

Ears get cold quickly especially if the wind is blowing. The jack rabbit from the USA and the fennec fox from the Sahara Desert use their huge ears to keep cool. Air blowing across the ears cools down the blood in the ears. The jack rabbit's ears can be 21 cm (8 in) long, a quarter of the total length of its body.

A duck-billed platypus has a beak similar to a bird's but it is soft. It uses its beak to sift mud for food and has a pair of nostrils near the tip. The beak has lots of very sensitive nerve endings and the platypus finds its food of worms and small fish by touch. Underwater, a platypus can cover its eyes and ears to stop water getting in.

Cats' eyes

At the back of a cat's eye there is a special layer which reflects light. This means that cats can make much better use of light than human beings. They can hunt well at night because they are able to see in very dim light.

Bat radar

Bats navigate and find food in the dark using sound. They make about 50 high squeaking noises a second. The sound hits a solid object and the bat's large sensitive ears pick up the echo. They seem to be able to tell the shape of an object by this echo.

In an experiment, bats used echo-location to fly through wires 30 cm (12 in) apart in total darkness without hitting them. If a bat's mouth is full it cannot squeak so some use their noses. Folds of skin called 'nose-leaves' around their noses direct sound like megaphones.

Star-nosed mole

Moles spend most of their lives underground searching for food. They have very poor eyesight but very sensitive noses. The star-nosed mole of North America has a strange rosette of 22 tentacles surrounding its nose. They help the mole find its way underground by touch.

Big nose

The African elephant has the biggest nose of any mammal. A large male's trunk is about 2.5 m (8 ft) from base to tip. The trunk is used for breathing, smelling and sucking up water. It also acts as an extra hand for picking up food and scratching. Elephants in Kenya's National Park even learnt to turn taps on with their trunks.

Tops and tails

Antlers and horns

Antlers are made of bone. They fall off every autumn and grow back in spring. Each year they get bigger and more branched. Usually only the males have antlers for fighting off rivals in the mating season. Horns are made of keratin which also makes hair. They grow throughout an animal's life.

Travellers' tails

A kangaroo uses its tail for balance. As it bounds along the ground, its body leans forward and its large tail is stretched out behind. In this way, a red kangaroo can leap over 7 m (25 ft) at a time, nearly four times the length of its body. Giant leaps of 12 m (40 ft) have been known.

Longest horns

The longest horns belong to the water buffalo in India. A huge bull shot in 1955 had horns which measured 4.24 m (14 ft) across from tip to tip.

Heavy headgear

The North American elk has the longest antlers of any animal. They can be up to 1.78 m (5.8 ft) long. The moose has the heaviest antlers. They can weigh as much as two heavy suitcases.

Amazing But True

Synthetoceras was a strange mammal which lived about 15 million years ago in North America. It looked like a deer but instead of antlers had two small horns on its forehead and a huge forked horn in the shape of a Y growing on its nose.

Getting the point

The white rhinoceros has a huge front horn. It can be up to 1.58 m (5 ft) long which is about three times as long as a human arm.

Rhinoceroses also have a shorter back horn. If the horns get broken off they will grow back at a rate of about ½ cm (¼ in) a month.

Secret weapon

The skunk's tail hides a very effective secret weapon. When it is threatened, the skunk lifts up its tail and squirts out a vile-smelling liquid from a gland hidden underneath. The terrible smell given off can reach up to ½ km (0.3 miles) away.

Useful tails

Squirrels make good use of their long, bushy tails. If they hibernate in winter they wrap their tails round them like fur coats to keep warm. The ground squirrel in the Kalahari Desert keeps cool by angling its tail over its head like a parasol.

Flying the flag

When ring-tailed lemurs are walking along the ground in search of food, each keeps its striped tail raised high in the air. This shows the others where each lemur is and keeps the group safely together.

Tree-top tails

Some mammals which spend their lives up in the tree-tops have 'prehensile' tails. This means the tail can be used as an extra arm or leg to grasp hold of the branches. Spider monkeys have such strong tails that they can easily support their whole body weight on their tail alone.

DID YOU KNOW?

The Asian elephant has the longest tail of any land mammal. Excluding the tuft of hair on the end, the tail can be up to 1.5 m (5 ft) long.

Mammal tails

Mammal	Body length	Tail length
Snow leopard	1.75 m	1.13 m
Jerboa	15 cm	30 cm
Red kangaroo	2 m	1.05 m
Giant anteater	1 m	60-90 cm
Long-tailed shrew	5-10 cm	3-8 cm
Spider monkey	40-62 cm	50-90 cm
Palm squirrel	11-18 cm	11-18 cm
Bottle-nosed dolphin	3-4 m	0.75 m (width)
Honey bear	1-1.2 m	5 cm
Hippopotamus	3-3.5 m	25-50 cm

Coats and camouflage

Warm coats

All mammals have some hair. It helps to keep them warm by stopping heat escaping from their bodies and helps protect them from injury. A mammal's coat usually has two sorts of hair – a soft underfur with longer 'guard hairs' on top. The colour of some coats helps hide the mammal from enemies and is also used for making signals.

Longest hair

Mammals that live in cold places have the longest hair. The musk ox in Greenland has hair 60-90 cm (24-35 in) long and can live in temperatures as low as −27°C (−60°F). Without its thick, warm coat it would freeze to death.

Hair flower

The hyrax has a very unusual hair 'flower'. On its back is a gland surrounded by long hairs of a different colour to its coat. When the hyrax is threatened these hairs stand on end so that the flower seems to 'bloom'.

Walrus whiskers

Some mammals have very sensitive whiskers which help them to find their way around in the dark or underwater. A walrus's moustache contains about 700 hairs. It uses these to feel its way around in murky water. The hairs may also be used as forks to hold shellfish in place while the walrus sucks out the soft insides.

Until the age of three months a cheetah cub has a thick mane of smoky-grey hair on its back. The mane is about 8 cm (3 in) long and helps hide the cub among dry grasses and bushes. Manes also make an animal look bigger and fiercer than it really is to scare away enemies.

Cunning colours

The patterned coats of mammals such as tapirs, tigers and giraffes help to hide them from enemies or to stalk their prey unnoticed. Their coats blend in with the patches of light and shadow in the jungles and grasslands where they live. The black and white coat of a Malayan tapir disguises it so well that, when it is lying on the forest floor, it looks like a harmless pile of stones.

Thick tufts

The tuft of hair at the end of an elephant's tail is about 20 cm (7½ in) long. Each hair can be up to 3 mm (0.1 in) thick, over 40 times thicker than human hair.

Hairy heirlooms

In the last Ice Age which ended 10,000 years ago, rhinoceroses and mammoths adapted to the freezing conditions by growing long, warm coats. Cave paintings show the woolly rhinoceros with a thick black and reddish coat. Whole mammoths have been found deep-frozen in the ground in Siberia with some of their coats still intact.

Pin cushion

Mammals' quills and prickles are types of hair but may be very hard and sharp. Some porcupines have quills up to 40 cm (16 in) long. A Canadian porcupine has about 30,000 quills each up to 12 cm (5 in) long. Put end to end, they would reach a third of the way up Mount Everest. When attacked, a porcupine charges backwards and sticks its quills into its enemy. As it moves forward again the quills are left behind causing serious wounds.

Amazing But True

A pangolin is covered in very unusual scales because they are actually made from hairs. When a pangolin is born the scales are soft but they soon harden and help to protect the pangolin from predators. Ordinary hair grows between the scales and on the underside of a pangolin's body.

Green hair

The sloth in South America hangs upside-down in trees. Unlike the hair of any other mammmal, a sloth's long hair grows from its stomach down towards its back. Sloths are so dirty that green algae grow on their coats This camouflages the sloth among the trees and is an ideal egg-laying site for some moths. The newly-hatched caterpillars feed on the algae.

Communication

Sights and sounds

Other mammals cannot speak as people do but communicate by smell, sight, sound and touch. Each species has different signals to warn others in the group of danger, mark its territory, call its young or find a mate.

Smelly signals

The tenrec, an insect-eater from Madagascar, spits on a spot it wants to mark, then rubs its hand along its side and on the wet place. It does this to mark its territory with its own strong body smell. Other tenrecs recognise the scent and are warned to stay away.

Tail talk

Dogs use their tails to show their feelings. A happy dog wags its tail. A frightened dog puts its tail between its legs. An angry cat, though, swishes its tail from side to side and holds it upright if it is content.

When two prairie dogs meet they exchange a sort of 'kiss' to find out if they know each other. If they do not, the intruder is driven away but if they do, they 'kiss' again and then start grooming each other. Prairie dog burrows are guarded by sentries who sound the alarm with a series of whistling barks if an enemy is seen.

Baby talk

Baby animals make signals. A baby orang-utan's small size, big eyes, high forehead and jerky movements all give out a special message. They tell the adults in the group that this is a baby who needs to be looked after.

Laughing hyena

Hyenas hunt together in teams and make many different noises for communication. They growl, grunt, whine and yelp but also burst into noisy choruses which sound like hysterical laughter. Only human beings can really laugh.

Body language

Chimpanzees are among the very few mammals which can pull faces to show their feelings. They can show anger, happiness and interest very much like human beings. But if a chimp seems to be grinning, showing its teeth, it is probably frightened, not smiling. Chimps also shake their fists to show anger, and cuddle and touch each other to show affection.

Whale of a song

Dolphins have a wide vocabulary of over 32 sounds. They use squeals, clicks, barks and whistles to 'talk' to each other. A dolphin uses different sounds to tell others in the group who it is, where it is and to warn them if there is danger. Dolphins also use sound as bats do to navigate and to find their food.

Whales build up series of sounds into 'songs'. A song may last for about ten minutes but some humpback songs lasting 30 minutes have been recorded. Some are sung over and over again for as long as 24 hours. Whales have very loud voices. Some are even louder than the sound of a jet plane.

Rousing chorus

Howler monkeys live high up in the tree tops in South American forests. To warn off enemies they make one of the loudest mammal sounds. Every morning and evening the monkeys sing in chorus, their throats swelling up like huge balloons. They can be heard about 8 km (5 miles) away.

Colour coded

Monkeys have very good eyesight and so can use colour to signal to others in their group or to enemies. Many have brightly-coloured hair and skin which show others which species they belong to and which sex they are.

Mandrill

The male mandrill's scarlet and blue face and bottom warn off rivals.

Uakari

The uakari has a red face which gets brighter if it is angry or excited.

De Brazza's monkey

These are part of a large group of monkeys called guenons. Colour is used

Moustached monkey

by the guenons to tell the difference between the many types.

Instinct and intelligence

Clever monkey

Most animals behave according to their instinct but some animals are also able to learn facts and work out problems. Monkeys and apes are among the most intelligent animals. Johnnie, a rhesus monkey living on a farm in Australia, learned to drive a tractor. He was also able to understand commands such as 'turn left' and 'turn right'.

Sign language

A 13-year old gorilla, called Koko, was taught from an early age to use sign language. She now knows about 1,000 words. Koko is very fond of her cat and describes him as 'Soft good cat cat' and herself as 'Fine animal gorilla'. In an intelligence test taken at the age of seven, Koko proved to be just as clever as a human seven-year old.

Some mammals use twigs or stones as tools. The sea otter floats on its back in the water with a large stone balanced on its stomach. It smashes shellfish against the stone to open them up to eat.

The otter keeps its face turned away to avoid being hit by sharp pieces of broken shell. One otter was seen to open 54 mussels in 86 minutes. It smashed them against a stone over 2,000 times.

Washing up

Macaques are very intelligent monkeys. Scientists studying a group of macaques in Japan, began to feed them with sweet potatoes. A year later they were amazed to see a 3½-year old female, Imo, dip her potato in a pool to wash off the sand. The others followed her lead but soon found that washing the food in the sea gave it a better, salty taste.

Going home

Some animals are able to find their way back home even over very long distances. In 1979 a doctor in the USSR found and looked after an injured hedgehog. She later gave it to her granddaughter who lived in another town. Two months later she found the hedgehog sitting on her doorstep again. It had walked 77 km (48 miles) back home, much further than a hedgehog would usually go.

Which way?

In the autumn mammals such as whales and bats make long journeys to warmer places to feed or breed. This is called migration. These animals seem to find their way there and back each year without getting lost. Scientists think they must have a built-in compass telling them which route to take.

A young artist, D. James Orang, won first prize in an art contest held in 1971 in Kansas, USA. His paintings sold well and he became quite famous. The judges did not realise that the painter was in fact a six-year old orang-utan, Djakarta Jim, living in Topeka Zoo.

More animal nomads

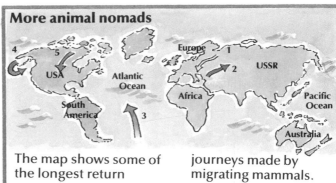

The map shows some of the longest return journeys made by migrating mammals.

⬆ 1 Noctule bat
2,300 km

⬆ 2 European pipistrelle
1,300 km

⬆ 3 Humpback whale
8,000 km

⬆ 4 Alaskan fur seal (male)
5,000 km

⬆ 5 Caribou
2,250 km

Sea marathon

The longest journey is made by grey whales. In late autumn they leave their feeding grounds in the Bering Sea and travel 9,650 km (6,000 miles) south along the west coast of the USA to Mexico. This is about the same distance as from London to Tokyo. In the spring they return north by the same route. The journey takes about 90 days.

Fast asleep

Instinct tells some mammals to hibernate during cold winters when food is scarce. Their breathing and pulse rates slow right down and their body temperature drops. Some live off fat stored in their bodies; others store food in their dens. Marmots hibernate for the longest time. They sleep for 7-8 months every year, losing about a quarter of their body weight.

Families and herds

Safety in numbers

Many mammals live in families or herds. They work together to defend themselves and search for food. Often the members of a group are closely related. A herd of antelopes may include parents and children, aunts, uncles and cousins. Animal groups often have definite leaders.

Job sharing

Mole rats in Africa have very well-organised family groups. One large female is the queen and has all the babies. The smaller mole rats do the hard work, digging tunnels and finding food. The larger rats are much lazier than this. They look after the nests for the young and sound the alarm if they see an intruder near the burrow.

The greatest gathering of any one type of mammal takes place on the Pribilof Islands in the Bering Sea. Each year about 1½ million Alaskan fur seals go there to breed, producing 500,000 pups.

Anti-social sloth

Some mammals live very solitary lives. The three-toed sloth spends 18 hours of its day asleep and the rest feeding, all by itself.

DO NOT DISTURB

Hunting packs

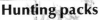

Wolves hunt in packs, following a set plan of attack. When tracking a moose, wolves set out in single file. Once a moose is sighted they stand very still, then suddenly rush towards it. As soon as it starts to run, the wolves attack. A large pack of about 16 wolves may track up to 12 moose before finally catching one.

Prairie dogs, or ground squirrels, live in vast systems of burrows called 'towns'. Each town is divided into smaller family units called 'coteries'. A prairie dog town found in Texas, USA in the 19th century contained an

incredible 400 million animals. It covered an area about twice the size of Belgium.

Bat caves

Bats are very sociable animals and live together in huge cave colonies. The largest bat colony in the world is in Bracken Cave, Texas, USA. During the summer the cave is the home of as many as 20 million Mexican free-tailed bats.

The largest herds ever recorded were those of springbok in southern Africa in the 19th century. When food and water became scarce, the springbok would set off in search of new pastures. The last great herd was seen in 1896. It is said to have covered 5,360 sq km (2,070 sq miles), over three times the area of London, England. There were over 10 million animals.

Some animal groups have very unusual names:
A clowder of cats
A leap of leopards
A sloth of bears
A skulk of foxes
A labour of moles
A crash of rhinoceroses
A trip of goats
A shrewdness of apes
A troop of kangaroos
A pride of lions
A pod of dolphins

Jumbo care

Elephants live in herds of 200 or more animals, led by female elephants. During the day the herd splits into smaller groups to feed and find water. The young are looked after by one or two mothers in 'nursery' groups. Females spend all their lives with the herd but single males sometimes leave and are then known as 'rogues' because they can become very fierce. If an elephant dies the herd mourns and stays by the body for several days, covering it with leaves and earth before they go away.

Mammals at home

Home, sweet home

The type of home a mammal has depends on how much protection it needs from predators and the weather, and if it needs a safe place for its young. Many mammals do not have fixed homes. They wander in search of food. Some live in one area, called a territory, which they defend against intruders.

Sea mammals have no fixed home in the water but some have special sleeping habits. Florida manatees sleep on the sea bed. They come to the surface every ten minutes or so to breathe. Sea otters sleep floating on the surface. They wind strands of seaweed round their bodies to stop themselves drifting.

Long sleep

Big cats, such as leopards, sleep for between 12-14 hours a day. They lie on the ground or stretch out along tree branches. They do not need shelters as they live in a warm climate and have no natural enemies.

Mouse house

A harvest mouse builds its nest among tall grasses. Large nests are about the size and shape of cricket balls. The mouse splits blades of grass into thin strips with its teeth and weaves them into a framework. The blades are still joined to the stalks so the nest is firmly wedged. The framework is padded out with more grass, feathers and even pieces of string.

Amazing But True

Burrows are the most common type of homes for small mammals. Mole rats are among the best burrowers. The Russian mole rat, digging with its teeth, can shift 50 times its own

weight of soil in about 20 minutes. Moles can dig a 2 m (6½ ft) long tunnel in about 12 minutes. At this rate it would take a mole only four years to dig its way from London to Paris.

Apes asleep

Chimpanzees and orang-utans sleep in flimsy, temporary nests up in the trees. It takes a chimp about five minutes to build a nest. It bends branches across to form a firm base and then weaves smaller twigs into it. If the night is cold, apes wrap themselves up in leaf or grass 'blankets'.

Escape routes

Rabbits dig large tunnel systems underground. The tunnels lead to living and sleeping rooms and nurseries. Above ground the rabbits dig out special 'bolt' holes which they stay close to when they are feeding outside. If there is danger, the rabbits bolt head first down the nearest hole to safety underground.

Houseproud badgers

Badgers live in setts made up of chambers with connecting tunnels. One of the largest setts known had 94 tunnels. The same sett may be used over and over again for as long as 250 years. Badgers are very houseproud. They line their bedrooms with bracken, moss and grass. On dry mornings they drag huge piles of bedding outside to air in the sun.

Master builders

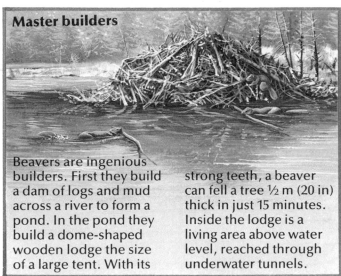

Beavers are ingenious builders. First they build a dam of logs and mud across a river to form a pond. In the pond they build a dome-shaped wooden lodge the size of a large tent. With its strong teeth, a beaver can fell a tree ½ m (20 in) thick in just 15 minutes. Inside the lodge is a living area above water level, reached through underwater tunnels.

Record breaker

Beaver dams are usually about 23 m (75 ft) long. The largest dam ever built is on the Jefferson River, USA. It is 700 m (2,296 ft) long and strong enough to bear the weight of a person riding across it on horseback.

Bear caves

Some bears hibernate in the winter when it is cold and food is scarce. They dig dens in the ground or find caves or hollow trees to live in. A female polar bear digs a den in the snow in October and has her cubs there. They leave the den in the spring.

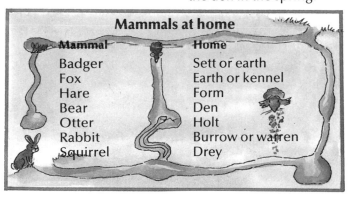

Mammals at home

Mammal	Home
Badger	Sett or earth
Fox	Earth or kennel
Hare	Form
Bear	Den
Otter	Holt
Rabbit	Burrow or warren
Squirrel	Drey

Runners

Fastest on land

Cheetahs are the fastest land mammals with a top speed of 115 kph (71 mph), as fast as an average car. They can only run fast for short distances though and have to rest after about 500 m (550 yards). Cheetahs have flexible backbones which allow

them to take giant 7 m (23 ft) leaps. They can reach 72 kph (45 mph) from a standstill in just two seconds. In the 1930s cheetahs were raced against greyhounds in London. The cheetahs won.

Let's dance

Sifakas, or white lemurs, of Madagascar spend a lot of their time high up in the tree tops. They can swing easily from tree to tree. Their legs are much longer than their 'arms' so running on all fours along the ground is impossible. Instead, they do a type of dance on their back legs. They bounce from one foot to the other, holding their arms high in the air.

Pronghorn puff

The fastest land mammal over long distances is the pronghorn antelope of the USA. It can keep up a speed of 45-50 kph (28-31 mph) for about 14 minutes and has a top speed of 85 kph (53 mph). A pronghorn can run fast for so long because it has very well-developed lungs and a heart twice as big as that of other animals of a similar size.

DID YOU KNOW?

The sloth is the slowest land mammal in the world with a top speed of only 2 kph (1.3 mph). It would take a sloth travelling at normal speed about 22 minutes to go 100 m (110 yards). The fastest man in the world can run this distance in under 10 seconds.

Top speeds

Cheetah	115 kph
Blackbuck	80 kph
Brown hare	72 kph
Race horse	69 kph
Greyhound	66 kph
Red fox	64 kph
Giraffe	51 kph
African elephant	40 kph
Arabian camel	32 kph
American porcupine	16 kph
House rat	9 kph
Common shrew	4 kph
Sloth	2 kph

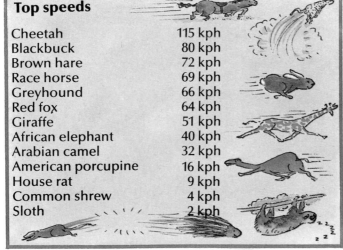

Climbers

Climbing aid

Some mammals have their own special ways of making climbing up tree trunks easier. The slow-moving Canadian porcupine has non-slip pads on the soles of its feet. It also has spines underneath its tail which help it to grip the tree trunk. An African spiny squirrel also has spines on its tail.

Sure-footed

Some mammals have specially adapted feet for climbing. Rocky Mountain goats in the USA are very sure-footed and can climb up nearly vertical slopes and walk safely along narrow ledges. Their hooves have sharp edges which dig into cracks in the rocks to give a secure foothold and their soles have hollows which stick to rocks like suction pads.

Amazing But True

One of the best mountain climbers was a beagle from Switzerland called Tschingel. From 1868-1876 she climbed 53 of the most difficult mountains in the Alps, 11 of which had never been climbed before, and many easier ones. In 1875 she climbed Mont Blanc, the highest mountain in the Alps and was made a member of the exclusive Alpine Club.

Short cut

Most big cats are good climbers but the puma has an easier way of getting up and down trees. It is an excellent jumper. From a standstill it can leap 7 m (23 ft) up into a tree and jump down to the ground from heights of up to 18 m (60 ft).

Speedy climber

The fastest animal mountain climber is the chamois, a mountain goat which lives in the Pyrenees and Alps in Europe. It can climb 1,000 m (3,280 ft) in only 15 minutes. At this rate a chamois could climb to the top of Mount Everest, the highest point on Earth, in just over two hours.

Swinging gibbons

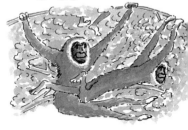

Some mammals do not need to climb well. A gibbon has arms twice as long as its body. The easiest way for it to move through the trees is to swing. Its armspan is about 2.1 m (7ft) and it can swing 12 m (39 ft) from one branch to the next, gripping the branches firmly with its long, curved fingers.

Flying mammals

Air-borne bats

Bats are the only mammals which can fly although some mammals can glide. There are over 900 different species. Bats are the second largest group of mammals, after rodents and make up one fifth of the world's mammals. Bats live all over the world, except in very cold places. There are two main groups – the large fruit bats or flying foxes, and the smaller insect-eaters. Some bats also feed on birds, lizards, fish, nectar and blood.

Nectar eaters

Jamaican flower bats and tube-nosed fruit bats eat nectar. They hover near flowers and stick their long tongues deep down inside to reach the food. Bats help to pollinate flowers. Pollen stuck to their bodies is carried to another flower.

Taking to the air

The Latin word for bats is 'chiroptera' which means 'hand-wings'. About 60 million years ago some insect-eating mammals developed into bats and their bodies became adapted for flight. A bat's wings have formed from its hands and arms. Its fingers are very long and support the skin stretched across them. The thumb is left free. The wing is also attached to the bat's back legs and often to its tail.

DID YOU KNOW?

Vampires are the most dangerous bats as they spread diseases such as rabies. There are many legends about vampires. In Eastern Europe it was thought that vampires were evil people who could turn into bats. To gain control over other people, they sucked their blood. Some ways of scaring away vampires were to show them a crucifix or to wear a necklace of garlic.

Bat ears

Bats have the best hearing of all land mammals. They have very sensitive and often very large ears which some use for locating their prey in the dark. The long-eared bat's body is only 5 cm (2 in) long but its ears are 4 cm (1½ in) long. If the bat was as big as a hare, its ears would be over 44 cm (1½ ft) long.

Bat homes

Bats feed at night and spend the day sleeping in caves or in tree tops. Some caves may be home to thousands of bats. Other bats make temporary shelters. They sleep under banana leaves, in empty burrows or even inside bamboo stems. Some South American bats make tent-like shelters out of palm tree leaves.

Catching fish

The hare-lipped bat in tropical America is an expert fisherman. It flies low over ponds and lakes. Spotting a fish just below the surface, it swoops down, raking the water with its large claws and scoops the fish up into its mouth. Its legs are not attached to the skin of its wings so they are free to act as fish hooks.

Bat facts

Largest	Bismarck flying fox
Smallest	Bumblebee bat
Most common	Typical small bats (pipistrelle; noctule bats)
Fastest flying	Brazilian free-tailed bat
Average life span	10-20 years
Average young	One baby or twins

Winter warmth

To avoid the cold winter months, some bats migrate to warmer places. Noctule bats travel the furthest, flying 2,300 km (1,430 miles) from Moscow to Bulgaria. Other bats hibernate in caves or in hollow tree trunks. Most hibernating mammals wake up every 10-20 days but brown bats sleep solidly for up to 66 days.

Flying lemurs

A few mammals are very good gliders though they cannot actually fly. Flying lemurs, or colugos, of the Far East are about the size of rabbits. Their front and back legs are joined by folds of furry skin down each side. The colugo spreads these out like wings and glides from tree to tree. It can glide for a distance of 91 m (300 ft) before landing.

Super gliders

Flying phalangers, such as the sugar glider, of Australia, and the flying squirrels of North America can also glide from tree to tree. Flying phalangers are in fact marsupials. They glide with their young in their pouches until the babies are two months old. Flying squirrels are rodents. They can glide as far as 450 m (⅓ mile).

Sea mammals

Sea mammals

There are over 4,000 species of mammals but only about 121 of these are sea mammals. Sea mammals are divided into three groups:

Pinnipedes – seals, sea-lions, walruses (32 species)
Sirenians (or sea cows) – manatees, dugongs (4 species)
Cetaceans – whales, dolphins, porpoises (about 85 species)

Sea unicorn

A narwhal has only two teeth which grow straight forward from its top jaw. The male's left tooth carries on growing in a spiral. It can be up to 2.5 m (9 ft) long. Narwhals are nearly extinct today because they were once hunted for their valuable tusks which were sold as unicorn horns. No one has yet found out what narwhals use their tusks for.

DID YOU KNOW?

The ancestors of sea mammals once lived on land. About 50 million years ago they began to return to the sea for food and their bodies adapted to life in the water. The whale's front legs became flippers, its back legs disappeared

and its nostrils became a blow-hole on top of its head. Sea mammals can hold their breath for a long time. A fin-back whale is able to stay underwater for 40 minutes; a bottle-nosed dolphin for two hours.

Seal tears

Seals lying on rocks out of the water often look as if they are crying. This is because they produce tears to keep their eyes moist. In the sea the tears get washed away but on land they trickle down the seals' cheeks.

Humpback acrobat

The humpback is the most athletic whale. It leaps high into the air and crashes down into the water on its back. It can even turn complete somersaults in the air. A humpback whale's body is often covered in barnacles which may weigh as much as eight people. The whale may leap to try and get rid of the weight.

Power propeller

The killer whale is the fastest sea mammal. It uses its strong tail as a propeller to speed it through the water. Thrashing its tail up and down, it can reach a top speed of about 65 kph (40 mph), eight times faster than the fastest human swimmer.

Whale blubber

Instead of fur, whales have a thick layer of fat, called blubber, round their bodies. Blubber keeps them warm and helps support their large bodies in the water. Some whales have blubber 38 cm (15 in) thick. Whales have long been hunted for the valuable oils in their blubber. A blue whale's blubber can weigh as much as four tractors and may contain over 120 barrels of oil.

Pinnipede records

Largest	Southern elephant seal
Smallest	Ringed seal
Fastest	Californian sea-lion
Deepest-diver	Weddell seal
Most common	Crabeater seal
Rarest	Monk seal

Amazing But True

The mermaid legend is thought to come from the rather ugly dugong. Close to, it is hard to believe that these lumbering creatures could have been mistaken for mermaids but from a distance they do look a little like human forms with fish-like tails.

Dolphin care

Some dolphins travel in family groups called pods, of up to 1,000 animals. If a dolphin is ill or wounded, the others push it to the surface so it can still breathe. A shark may be able to kill a single dolphin but if it attacks a pod, the dolphins ram it with their 'beaks'. They scare the shark off and may even kill it.

Walking teeth

In the breeding season huge herds of walruses gather on islands in the Bering Sea. Adults, which can weigh over a tonne, use their tusks to drag themselves over the land. The Latin name for walrus, *Odobenus rosmarus*, actually means 'the one who walks with its teeth'.

Mammals of the cold

Out in the cold

Mammals living in very cold places need special survival skills. Many have thick coats for keeping warm and broad feet for walking on ice and snow. The vicuña, a relation of the camel, lives in the Andes in South America. It has such a warm coat that it can even overheat. But it also has bare patches on its legs. To cool down, it turns so that these are facing the wind.

High home

The highest-living mammal is the wild yak of Tibet and China. It can climb to heights of over 6,000 m (20,000 ft) in search of food. Its long, thick blackish coat protects it from the biting cold. People in Nepal keep domestic yaks for milk, wool and dung for fuel.

Snowshoe rabbit

Snowshoe rabbits in North America get their name from their broad feet. These act like snowshoes and stop the rabbit sinking in the deep snow. Long hairs grow on the sides of the feet and between the toes. They keep the rabbit's feet warm and help them to grip the frozen ground.

DID YOU KNOW?

Macaques living high up in the mountains of northern Japan have to cope with very harsh winters. They keep warm by taking long baths in the hot, volcanic springs nearby.

Cool cats

The rare snow leopard, or ounce, lives in the mountains of Central Asia. It has a thick, smoky-grey coat with black rosette markings. In summer the snow leopard lives nearly 6,000 m (20,000 ft) up in the mountain peaks. In winter it comes down to the lower slopes below 3,000 m (10,000 ft) in search of food.

All change

The Arctic fox, some stoats and the snow hare change colour as the seasons change. They have brown summer coats, moult in autumn and turn white in winter. Throughout the year they blend in with the countryside and are very well hidden from hungry predators.

Mountain mammals

The list shows the maximum heights at which various mammals are found.

By comparison, Mount Everest, the highest point on Earth, is 8,848 m tall.

Tibetan antelope
6,000 m — Woolly hare
5,800 m — Mongolian wolf
5,600 m — Puma
5,500 m — Brown bear
4,700 m — Snow vole
3,600 m — Red panda

Deep-sea diver

The Weddell seal lives in the Antarctic, further south than any other mammal. It spends most of its time under the pack ice, kept warm by a thick layer of fat under its skin. It chews holes in the ice to reach air to breathe.

Hardy huskies

Husky dogs are among the hardiest animals. They have thick coats and can live in temperatures as low as −45°C (−50°F) without shelter. They are also very strong. A team of 12 can pull a sled weighing half a tonne, as much as eight people and their luggage.

Amazing But True

Polar bears are sometimes seen on land. A teacher at a school near the northerly Kara Sea, USSR, heard the door bell ring and went to answer it. She found that the caller was a huge polar bear leaning on the door bell.

Abominable snowman

Many people claim to have seen yetis in the Himalayas. They are supposed to be ape-like creatures with long, shaggy coats. In 1951 photographs of yeti footprints were published but no one has proved yetis exist. It is thought that yetis are, in fact, large black or brown bears. A more unusual explanation is that they are 'visions' or hallucinations caused by a lack of oxygen at high altitudes.

Ice bear

The largest polar mammal is the polar bear. The heaviest recorded weighed over a tonne. Polar bears live on the pack ice near the North Pole. This is the bear's hunting ground. It waits by an air-hole for a seal to surface and kills it with a blow of its paw. Polar bears are strong swimmers but prefer to use pieces of ice as rafts.

Mammals of the desert

Desert life

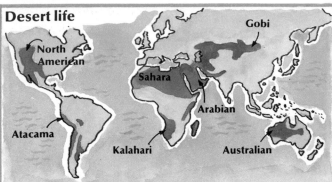

Deserts have less than 25 cm (10 in) of rain a year. They cover about a fifth of the Earth's land surface. Deserts are sandy, rocky or covered in stones and gravel. The Sahara Desert is almost as big as the whole USA. The temperature there may reach 57°C (134°F) during the day and drop well below freezing at night. Many plants and animals live in deserts. They all face the same problem – finding enough water to stay alive.

Plant food

Desert plants provide food and water for many animals. Cacti store water in their leaves and stems. Giant saguaro cacti in the North American deserts can weigh as much as 10 tonnes of which 9 tonnes may be water. Mammals eat the plants and seeds and can get enough water from them to live without drinking.

Underground cool

Most small desert mammals spend the day underground to avoid the heat. Scientists studying gerbil burrows in the Kara-Kum Desert, USSR, found that just 10 cm (4 in) below ground the temperature was 17°C (61°F) cooler than above. Mammals' breathing helps keep the burrows moist. In the day the burrow entrance is blocked to stop moisture escaping.

Sand survivor

The rare addax, a type of antelope, lives among the sanddunes in the southern Sahara. It is one of the few large mammals that can survive such harsh conditions. The addax never needs to drink. It gets all its moisture from the plants it eats.

DID YOU KNOW?

About 5,000 years ago the Sahara Desert was covered in rich grassland and trees. Paintings found in caves in Tassili, Algeria, which date from about that time, show giraffe, hippopotamus and lions, people hunting and cattle grazing.

Living in the desert

Here are some of the ways mammals have of coping with the desert heat and lack of water:

1. Hunt only during cooler night
2. Sweat very little so lose little water
3. Get water from the plants and seeds they eat
4. Concentrated urine so body loses less water
5. Large ears which give off excess heat
6. Small mammals spend day in cool burrows

Kit fox

The kit fox hunts for food at night, well hidden by its greyish-black coat. It has excellent hearing for detecting its prey in the dark. It also loses heat through its large ears to keep cool and they are lined with thick hair to keep out dust and sand.

Spit and polish

Desert wallabies and kangaroos in Australia have an unusual way of keeping cool. When it gets very hot they pant and make a lot of saliva. They lick the saliva over their bodies and rub their faces with their wet paws.

Little leaper

Kangaroo rats are an important part of desert life. They are often eaten by other animals for the water in their bodies. The rats can hop very fast to avoid their enemies, covering 6 m (20 ft) in one second. They use their long tails as rudders when jumping and can even change their course in mid-air.

Sleepy squirrel

The Mojave squirrel in the USA survives long droughts by sleeping for whole days at a time in its underground burrow. Sleeping through hot, dry weather is called aestivation. The squirrel saves energy and is out of the heat.

Ships of the desert

There are two types of camel – the one-humped Arabian camel and the two-humped Bactrian camel. Both are well equipped for desert life. A camel's hump can weigh up to 13.5 kg (30 lb) and contains fat which can be used when there is no food. Camels can survive for many days without food and water. After a drought they will drink up to 114 litres (25 gallons) of water in one go.

Worlds apart

Australia's animals

Because Australia has been cut off from the rest of the world for over 60 million years, it has very unusual animals. Almost all its mammals are marsupials (mammals with pouches). There are over 150 kinds of Australian marsupials from tiny marsupial mice and moles to marsupial cats. Outside Australia marsupials are only found in South America with just one species in North America.

Honey possum

A honey possum, or noolbenger, of Western Australia, is about the size of a mouse. It has a special way of eating nectar and pollen. Its long tongue is covered in bristles with a tip like a tiny brush. Pollen sticks to the brush as it feeds.

Some unusual marsupials

Boodie

Member of the rat kangaroo family.

Numbat

Also called a banded anteater.

Quoll

A marsupial cat.

Bandicoot

Pouch opens to rear. Latin name means 'badger with a pouch'.

Amazing But True

The biggest collection of marsupial fossils was found in the Naracoorte Caves, Australia, in 1969. They showed giant marsupials including a creature the size of a rhinoceros. It probably died out about 40,000 years ago.

Wombat digger

Wombats are about the same size and shape as badgers. They are expert diggers and live in huge underground burrows surrounded by a maze of tunnels. A wombat's pouch opens backwards so that the baby being carried inside is not showered with earth as the wombat digs.

Marsupial records

Biggest	Red kangaroo	Up to 2.13 m tall
Smallest	Ingram's planigale	9 cm long
Fastest	Red kangaroo	48 kph
Rarest	Marsupial wolf	Last known died 1933.
Most common	Kangaroo	Over 50 species
Longest-lived	Common wombat	26 years

Madagascar

Madagascar is a huge island off the east coast of Africa. It is bigger than France. About 30 million years ago it became separated from Africa. Nine-tenths of the island's animals and plants are found nowhere else in the world. Its most famous mammals are lemurs which are related to monkeys and apes.

DID YOU KNOW?

The sportive lemur gets its name because, if attacked, it raises its fists like a boxer and punches its enemy. It feeds on Somy tree flowers. The tree is covered in sharp spikes but the lemur does not seem to hurt itself as it leaps from stem to stem.

Rousing chorus

The indri, the largest of the lemurs, lives mostly high up in the tree tops. It uses sound to scare away enemies and call its young. Every morning and evening, families of indris break into wailing songs. Each indri joins in at a different time so the strange chorus may last for many minutes.

Sun worship

Sifakas, or white lemurs, start off each day by lying in the sun for an hour or so. They climb to a tree top and face the sun with their arms outstretched. They do this to warm themselves up after a cool night but local people believed that the lemurs were worshipping the sun.

Fat store

Dwarf lemurs are amongst the smallest of the lemurs. The fat-tailed dwarf lemur eats insects, leaves and sap. During the rainy season it builds up a fat store under its skin and in its tail. It lives off this supply in the dry season when food is scarce.

Tenrecs

Another group of mammals found only in Madagascar are tenrecs. There are about 20 species of these small insect-eaters. Some have bristly coats like hedgehogs, others have fur. The common tenrec is the largest insect-eater in Madagascar. It may be as much as 40 cm (16 in) long, about the same size as a cat.

Mammals in danger

Under threat

Over 550 species of mammals are in danger of dying out for ever. When an animal species dies out, it is said to be extinct. If it is likely to die out unless it is protected, it is said to be endangered or threatened.

Why in danger

Many mammals become endangered because their homes are destroyed by farmers or foresters or they are hunted for their meat or fur. The South American rain forests contain about half of the world's plant and animal species. As they are destroyed to make room for farms or buildings, thousands of species are lost. It is thought that a piece of rain forest the size of Switzerland is cut down each year.

Run, rhino, run

All five species of rhinoceros are listed as endangered. Rhinos have long been hunted for their horns. A powder made from horn was thought to cure fevers and headaches. In 1978 there were about 140,000 rhino in the wild. Ten years later this number had been reduced to 14,000.

Giant panda

Giant pandas once lived all over China but are now only found in the south-west. Pandas live mainly on bamboo. If this dies or is cut down, they may starve. In 1981 the World Wildlife Fund and the Chinese Government started the project 'Save the Panda' to protect them.

DID YOU KNOW?

In 1700 there were some 60 million buffalo in North America. Millions were killed for their meat and because their grazing land was needed for farming. By 1880 there were only a few hundred left. Today the buffalo are making a slow comeback. There are now about 10,000 in the wild.

Operation tiger

Many of the big cats, including the Asian lion, the leopard and the tiger, are endangered. In 1945 there were over 100,000 tigers in India; by 1970 probably about 4,000 were left. Tigers were hunted for their fur and for sport. Today there are special tiger reserves in India and tigers are now strictly protected by law.

Monkeys and apes

Some endangered mammals

Mountain gorilla (Africa)	Less than 400 left in the wild.
Arabian oryx	Last seen in the wild in 1972. Now being re-introduced.
Indian lion	Hunted and forest home destroyed.
African elephant	Over 50,000 killed a year for the ivory from their tusks.
Grey whale (North Pacific)	Migration routes and breeding grounds destroyed by ships.
Baiji dolphin (China)	Less than 400 left; the most threatened whale species.
Sea otter (North Pacific)	Hunted for valuable fur; hunting now banned.

The golden lion tamarin is one of the world's rarest monkeys. Only about 200 still survive in patches of forest in Brazil. Much of the monkey's forest home has been cleared to make way for sugar cane and coffee plantations and for building. One fifth of all the species of monkeys and apes in the world are endangered, including proboscis monkeys, black gibbons, chimpanzees and orang-utans.

How to help

Unless human beings stop destroying habitats and polluting water, mammals such as blue whales and polar bears could become extinct by the beginning of the next century. The World Wildlife Fund was set up in 1961 to help protect the world's animals. It now has over 4,000 conservation projects in over 135 countries round the world. Groups like this and laws banning hunting or poaching have helped save some of the mammals most at risk.

Unsafe seas

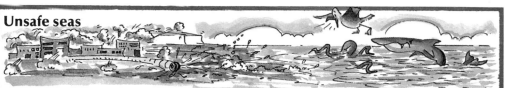

As the seas become more polluted, many sea mammals are in danger of dying out. Chemical waste, sewage and oil spilt from tankers kill the mammals' food supplies. Seals and whales are also hunted for their meat and skins. Today they are protected but some are still killed. It is thought that there are now only 500 Mediterranean monk seals left and that the Caribbean monk seal may be extinct.

The smallest mammals

Smallest on land

The smallest land mammal is the tiny Savi's pygmy shrew which lives in southern Europe and Africa. It is 3.8 cm (1½ in) long with a tail which measures 2.5 cm (1 in). A fully-grown shrew weighs only about as much as a table tennis ball.

Smallest meat eater

The dwarf or least weasel which lives in Siberia is the smallest carnivore. An adult measures 17-20 cm (6.6-7.8 in) in length. It weighs about as much as ten lumps of sugar.

Pencil legs

The royal antelope which lives in West Africa is the smallest antelope in the world. Adults are only 25-30 cm (10-12 in) tall and weigh about 3-3.6 kg (7-8 lb). A royal antelope living in the London Zoo was said to have had legs thinner than pencils. Its hooves were so tiny that it was able to stand in a teaspoon with room to spare.

DID YOU KNOW?

The very rare bumblebee bat from Thailand is the smallest flying mammal. Adults have a wingspan of about 160 mm (6.3 in), about the same as that of a large butterfly. They weigh about as much as five drawing pins.

Smallest at sea

The smallest mammal in the seas is the Commerson's dolphin. An adult weighs 25-35 kg (55-77 lb), 3,500 times lighter than a blue whale, the largest sea mammal.

Miniature monkeys

The world's smallest primate is the lesser mouse lemur which lives on the island of Madagascar. When it is fully grown, it is about 11 cm (4.3 in) long, with a 15 cm (6 in) long tail. It

weighs only 50 g (1.7 oz). The tiny pygmy marmoset which lives in South America comes a close second. It weighs up to 75 g (2.6 oz), about as much as a hen's egg.

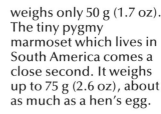

More small fry

Group	Smallest	Average weight (adult male)
Cat family	Rusty-spotted cat	1.35 kg
Seals	Ringed seal	127 kg
Deer	Northern pudu	7-8 g
Rodents	Northern pygmy mouse	7-8 kg
Domestic cat	Singapura	1.8 kg
Freshwater mammal	Southern water shrew	7.5-16 g
Bears	Malay bear	25-40 kg

Pocket sized

The very rare Ingram's planigale, a type of pouched mouse found only in north-west Australia, is the smallest marsupial in the world. Its body and head are 45 mm (1.7 in) long, its tail the same length again and it weighs only a little more than an airmail envelope.

The smallest dogs

The smallest breed of dogs is the chihuahua but the smallest dog ever known was a Yorkshire terrier. It died in 1945 aged two years. It was 6.3 cm (2½ in) tall at the shoulder, only 9.5 cm (3¾ in) from its nose to its tail and weighed an incredible 113 g (4 oz), about the same size as a hamster.

Mini horse

The smallest breed of horse is the Falabella from Argentina. Adults are less than 76 cm (30 in) tall. The smallest horse ever known was a tiny stallion called Little Pumpkin from the USA. Fully grown, it was only about the size of a small dog.

Amazing But True

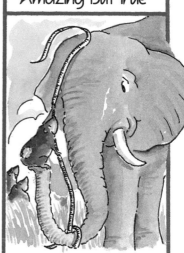

The closest relation to the African elephant, the world's largest living land mammal, is said to be the comparatively tiny hyrax. Hyraxes are about the size of rabbits but in prehistoric times they were almost as large as cows. Elephants and hyraxes are thought to have come from the same group of mammals, millions of years ago.

The biggest mammals

Sea giant

The biggest mammal that has ever lived is the gigantic blue whale. A female caught in the South Atlantic in 1922 was over 33 m (110 ft) long, nearly 1½ times as long as an Olympic swimming pool. Blue whales are also the heaviest mammals in the world. A single whale can weigh as much as 130 tonnes, over 20 times heavier than a bull (male) African elephant and almost as heavy as 2,000 men.

Amazing But True

A blue whale calf is the biggest mammal baby. When it is born, a calf can be over 7 m (25 ft) long and weigh nearly 2 tonnes. By drinking up to 600 litres (132 gallons) of its mother's rich milk a day it can double its weight in just a week. By the time it is seven months old, a calf may weigh as much as 23 tonnes.

Largest on land

The biggest land mammal in the world is the African elephant. An adult bull (male) is usually about 3 m (10½ ft) tall and weighs some 5½ tonnes. The largest African elephant ever recorded was about 4 m (13 ft) tall and weighed over 12 tonnes, as much as 16 average-sized cars.

Skyscraper

With its long neck and legs, the giraffe is the tallest mammal on Earth. An adult Masai giraffe bull can be over 5 m (17 ft) tall. A tall man would only come up to the top of its leg. The tallest giraffe ever recorded in the world was 5.87 m (19 ft 3 in) tall.

Gentle giant

The largest ape is the mountain gorilla in Africa. An average male stands 1.75 m (5 ft 9 in) tall and weighs about 195 kg (430 lb), with a massive chest of 1.5 m (5 ft). Gorillas are very gentle but very strong. Scientists have worked out that a two-year old gorilla's arms are about three times stronger than a two-year old child's.

Wonder wings

The largest flying mammal is the Bismarck flying fox, a bat from New Guinea. Its head and body are only 45 cm (18 in) long, but it can measure 1.6 m (5½ ft) across its outstretched wings, 2½ times the wingspan of a pigeon.

DID YOU KNOW?

The sperm whale has the heaviest mammal brain. Its brain weighs up to 9 kg (20 lb), six times heavier than a human brain. The whale has a very large head, about a third of its body length, so there is plenty of room for its big brain.

Biggest rodent

The capybara in South America is the world's largest rodent. It is about the size of a sheep, weighing up to 113 kg (250 lb). A harvest mouse, one of the smallest rodents in the world, is over 18,000 times lighter than its heavyweight relation.

Heavyweights

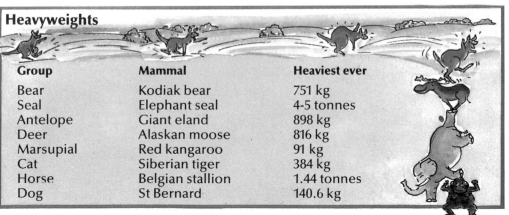

Group	Mammal	Heaviest ever
Bear	Kodiak bear	751 kg
Seal	Elephant seal	4-5 tonnes
Antelope	Giant eland	898 kg
Deer	Alaskan moose	816 kg
Marsupial	Red kangaroo	91 kg
Cat	Siberian tiger	384 kg
Horse	Belgian stallion	1.44 tonnes
Dog	St Bernard	140.6 kg

Habitat map

The type of place a mammal lives in is called its habitat. The larger map shows six main habitats and some of the animals found in them.

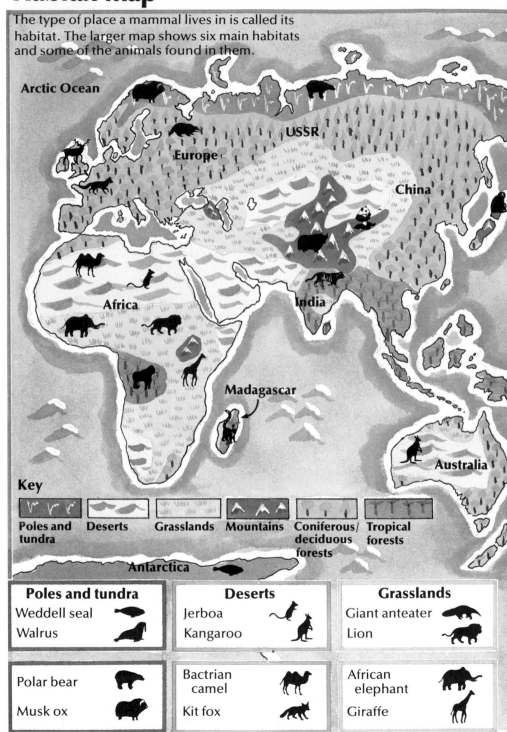

Arctic Ocean

USSR

Europe

China

Africa

India

Madagascar

Australia

Key

Poles and tundra	Deserts	Grasslands	Mountains	Coniferous/ deciduous forests	Tropical forests

Antarctica

Poles and tundra		**Deserts**		**Grasslands**	
Weddell seal		Jerboa		Giant anteater	
Walrus		Kangaroo		Lion	
Polar bear		Bactrian camel		African elephant	
Musk ox		Kit fox		Giraffe	

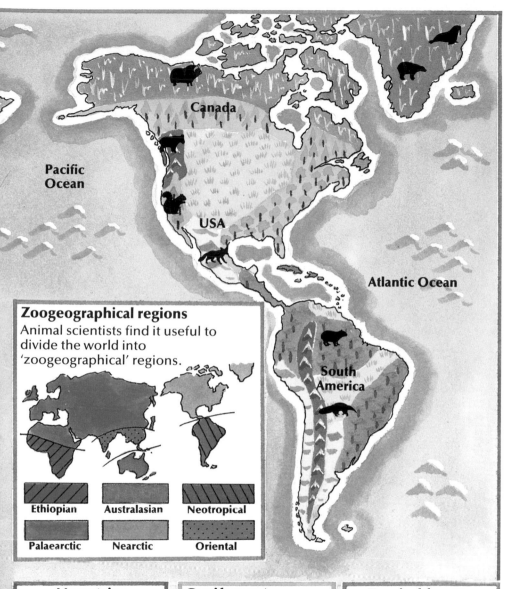

Pacific Ocean

Canada

USA

Atlantic Ocean

Zoogeographical regions

Animal scientists find it useful to divide the world into 'zoogeographical' regions.

South America

Ethiopian

Australasian

Neotropical

Palaearctic

Nearctic

Oriental

Mountains	
Yak	
Giant panda	

Coniferous/ deciduous forests	
Red deer	

Tropical forests	
Indian tiger	
Capybara	

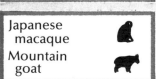
Japanese macaque

Mountain goat

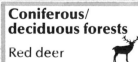
Grey squirrel

Red fox

European badger

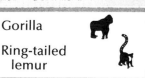
Gorilla

Ring-tailed lemur

Glossary

Adaptation Special characteristics to help animals survive. For example, Arctic mammals have very thick, warm fur to protect them from the cold.

Aestivation A time of inactivity or deep sleep to save energy and keep cool during very hot and dry weather.

Camouflage Some mammals have special colouring or markings which help disguise them and hide them from their enemies.

Carnivore An animal that only or mainly eats meat.

Conservation Protecting rare animals from becoming extinct.

Endangered Animals in danger of becoming extinct or dying out.

Evolution Animals gradually change over a very long time to become better suited to the way in which they live (depending on food supplies, habitat and climate).

Extinct Animals that no longer exist. They become officially extinct if there have been no certain records of them for 50 years.

Gestation The length of time of a mammal's pregnancy.

Habitat The type of place an animal lives in, for example, desert, jungle, mountain, grassland.

Herbivore An animal such as an elephant that mostly or only eats plants.

Hibernation A deep sleep or time of inactivity to save energy during the cold, winter months.

Marsupial Mammals with pouches. Their young are born tiny and ill-formed. They feed and grow further inside their mother's pouch.

Migration A return journey made by some mammals every year to a place for feeding or breeding.

Monotreme A mammal which lays eggs such as the duck-billed platypus and spiny anteater. The most primitive group of mammals.

Nocturnal Animals such as bats that are active at night when they hunt for food and rest during the day.

Omnivore Animals that eat both plants and meat.

Placental mammal The young develop fully inside the mother's body before they are born.

Predator A hunting animal that kills other animals for food.

Primates The group of mammals that includes monkeys, apes and man. Their special features include a large brain, and fingers (and sometimes toes) designed for grasping.

Territory An area which an animal or group of animals 'owns' and defends against other animals.

Vertebrate An animal with a backbone and an internal skeleton. Fish, amphibians, reptiles, birds and mammals are all vertebrates.

Warm-blooded Animals that can control their own body temperature so it stays the same whatever the weather outside, allowing them to be active in the heat or cold.

Index

BIRD FACTS

Bridget Gibbs

CONTENTS

Illustrated by Tony Gibson and Stephen Lings

Designed by Tony Gibson

**Consultant: Rob Hume,
Editor of *BIRDS* magazine, published by
The Royal Society for the Protection of Birds**

What is a bird?

How many birds?

There are about 8,600 different kinds, or species, of birds in the world. These are split into 28 groups called orders. More than half of all living birds are in the songbirds group.

Marathon fliers

Many birds can quickly travel vast distances to take advantage of the seasons and the best supplies of food. This movement is called migration. The champion migrant is the Arctic tern. It covers a round trip of 40,000km (25,000 miles) from the Arctic to the Antarctic and back. Terns can live for more than 20 years.

Featuring feathers

Birds are the only animals with feathers. When you look at a perched bird, most of the feathers you see are small ones that give its body a warm, smooth covering. When flying, birds show the larger, stiffer wing feathers used for flight.

DID YOU KNOW?

Wheatears living in Greenland are larger than those found further south. Being larger helps the birds to survive cold and longer migration flights to central Africa. The farther north a bird lives, the larger it tends to be.

Waterproof birds

Ducks, swans and most sea birds spend months on water and many birds dive underwater in search of food, but they never get wet through to the skin. They coat their feathers with oil from a special gland and constantly preen to keep feathers overlapping like tiles on a roof.

Running scared

Some birds run rather than fly from danger. The wild turkey, hoopoe lark and red-legged partridge all fly quite well, but prefer to sprint short distances to get away from people or predators.

Lightest and least

Birds are the only animals with hollow bones. This makes their skeletons the lightest for their size of any animal. They have fewer bones than mammals, but they have more neck bones. Nearly all mammals, even giraffes, have seven bones in their necks. Herons have about 16 and swans have as many as 25.

Features of birds

All birds have:
Feathers
Wings (though a few, such as ostriches, cannot fly)
Hollow bones (except for some flightless and diving birds)
Beaks
All birds lay eggs

The orders* of living birds

Runners and walkers	Number of species
Ostrich	1
Rheas	2
Cassowaries, emus	4
Kiwis	5
Fliers	
Tinamous	about 50
Penguins**	18
Divers	4
Grebes	about 20
Albatrosses, petrels	90
Pelicans, gannets, cormorants	about 59
Herons, storks, ibises, flamingos	118
Ducks, geese, swans	149
Vultures, hawks, eagles, falcons	287
Pheasants, grouse, megapodes	about 265
Cranes, rails, bustards	176
Oystercatchers, plovers, sandpipers, gulls, terns	320
Pigeons	271
Cockatoos, parrots	330
Cuckoos	128
Turacos	22
Owls	146
Nightjars	95
Swifts, hummingbirds	about 400
Mousebirds	6
Trogons	about 35
Kingfishers, bee-eaters, hoopoes	196
Woodpeckers, toucans, barbets	about 400
Songbirds and perching birds (from warblers to crows)	4,800

*An order is a group. (See top of previous page.)
**Penguins have become flightless. They use their wings to swim.

Birds of the past

The bird pioneer

The earliest known bird-like creature is Archaeopteryx, which lived about 150 million years ago. Fossils show that it had feathers, a wishbone and wings like a bird, but that it also had teeth, claws on its wings and a long, bony tail like a reptile.

What a water carrier

Ancient shells of elephant bird eggs were at one time used to carry water by people in Madagascar. The giant, emu-like bird produced the largest eggs ever known, equivalent in size to 180 hen's eggs.

Dinosaur descendants?

The existence of Archaeopteryx and other creatures, with their combination of bird and reptile features, has shown that birds may be the living descendants of dinosaurs.

Amazing But True

The largest bird ever to fly was *Argentavis magnificens* with a vast, 7.6m (25ft) wingspan. It probably did not flap its wings to fly but soared like a glider, much as South American condors do today.

Where eagles dared

The Haast eagle of New Zealand was a giant eagle with a wingspan of up to 3m (10ft). It preyed on other giants, the flightless moas. The biggest of these stood about 3m (10ft) high. The last Haast eagle died more than 500 years ago, but there may still have been some moas living in the 1800s.

Bird heavyweight

The heaviest bird of all time was *Dromornis stirtoni.* It weighed an amazing 500kg (over half a ton). This is nearly four times heavier than an ostrich, which is the largest living bird. It lived in Australia about 10 million years ago, but survived until about 25,000 years ago. Not surprisingly, Dromornis was a flightless bird.

The dawning of birds

Some of the earliest true birds were sea birds. One of these, Hesperornis, was nearly 2m (6ft) long. Its wings seem to have been almost non-existent, but its very strong legs must have made it a powerful swimmer. Unlike modern birds it had teeth.

DID YOU KNOW?

The passenger pigeon made the most rapid disappearance ever known. In the 1800s it was so common in the USA that flocks of over 2,000 million birds were estimated. By 1900 there were none left in the wild, and the last one died in a zoo in 1914.

Too tasty by half

The great auk was a big sea bird with tiny wings and quite incapable of flight. Sadly, man's greed caused it to become extinct by 1844. Both its single egg and its flesh were regarded as excellent food. Its oil was used as lamp fuel and even its feathers were valued.

When early birds lived

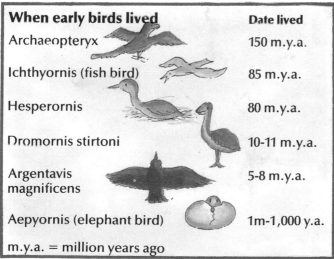

	Date lived
Archaeopteryx	150 m.y.a.
Ichthyornis (fish bird)	85 m.y.a.
Hesperornis	80 m.y.a.
Dromornis stirtoni	10-11 m.y.a.
Argentavis magnificens	5-8 m.y.a.
Aepyornis (elephant bird)	1m-1,000 y.a.

m.y.a. = million years ago

Feather care and flight

Zippy feathers

The parts of a feather (called vanes) either side of the central shaft, are kept in shape by a system of hooks. Each vane is made up of barbs. These are held together by tiny hooks. When ruffled, a feather has only to be drawn through the bird's beak to zip the barbs together again.

How many feathers?

Feathers make up about one sixth of a bird's weight. Hummingbirds have fewest feathers, some having less than 1,000. Some swans have more than 25,000. But hummingbirds have more feathers per square centimetre than swans.

Moulting

Feathers become worn with use and are usually replaced every year. In most birds, the shedding of feathers, called moulting, is gradual, so they are still able to fly reasonably well. Ducks and geese moult all their wing feathers at once in the autumn and are unable to fly for two to four weeks.

Herons have special feathers that break up into powder. They rub this into feathers that are sticky with slime from feeding on eels. The resulting sticky balls are then removed with tiny comb-like teeth on the middle claw of each foot.

Flight patterns

Birds have different ways of flying. Large birds soar in spirals, small birds often have bouncing flight, and others fly fast and straight.

Buzzard

Chaffinch

Mallard

Fastest fliers

The fastest level flight so far reliably timed is that of the eider duck at 76kph (42mph). But the peregrine, a falcon that dives on to its prey in mid-air from a great height, can reach speeds of at least 180kph (112mph) in a dive.

Featherless freeze

Penguins seem unable to move at all when they are moulting. The emperor penguin stands on the ice for three to five weeks while its old feathers fall out in big patches. During this time, it does not eat.

Amazing But True

In 1973 a Ruppell's griffon vulture collided with an aeroplane flying at 11,270m (37,000ft) over the coast of western Africa. This is the highest altitude at which any bird has been identified. The usual height for this vulture is up to 1,500m (5,000ft).

Flying speeds
Level flight in calm air

Bewick's swan	72kph
Mallard	65kph
Pheasant	54kph
Cedar waxwing	46kph
Grey heron	43kph
Swift	40kph
Starling	35kph
House sparrow	30kph

Fishy business

Baby grebes are fed on fish, but their parents also feed them feathers from their own bodies. The feathers may prevent fish bones injuring the baby grebes' stomachs.

Drying out?

Cormorants often stand on sandbanks or breakwaters with their wings held out. They do not have completely waterproof plumage and may do this to dry out.

Plumage

Camouflage

The plumage of many birds blends with their background and helps to hide them from enemies.

Tawny frogmouth looks like a tree stump.

Bitterns pose like this to blend in with reeds.

Ringed plover is hard to spot on a pebbly beach.

Changing colour

Plumage may change colour from wear and tear. In autumn, the plumage of the male black lark of Asia is mottled. During the year the pale tips of the black feathers crumble away, so by spring the bird's plumage is black.

Seasonal switch

Ptarmigans live in the Arctic and on high mountains. To provide year-round camouflage, their plumage changes colour with the seasons. In spring it is mottled brown to blend with plants, in autumn it is grey to look like rocks and in winter it is white to match the snow.

Take terns

The colour of a bird's plumage can play a part in its search for food. Terns and many other fish-eating sea birds have white underparts. Unsuspecting fish cannot see them against the bright sky.

DID YOU KNOW?

The pink colouring of flamingos depends on the food they eat. In the wild, they filter shrimps and algae from water. In captivity, they are often fed on carrot juice to prevent their feathers fading to dull grey.

Noisy tails

Male snipes have a noisy way of showing a mate that they have found a nesting place. They fly over the site, then dive down with their stiff outer tail feathers spread out each side. These special feathers vibrate in the air, making a loud, whirring noise known as drumming.

The highly ornamental phoenix fowl is bred for shows in Japan. Its fantastically long tail coverts* grow for about six years without a moult. The longest ever recorded were 10.59m (34.75ft), which is about as long as a bus.

Longest and shortest

The resplendent quetzal of Central America has magnificent, emerald green tail feathers. Over 60cm (24in) long, they are more than twice its body length. At the other extreme, birds such as kiwis and emus look tailless, having no special tail feathers.

Bouncing bishops

The red bishop of African plains is pale brown for most of the year. To find a mate, his plumage changes to black and red, and he fluffs out his feathers making him look like a brilliantly coloured ball. He then "bounces" over the grassland in a strange, bounding flight.

Follow their leader

Brent geese migrate in flocks from Siberia to Europe. To make sure they keep together and do not lose sight of one another, the birds have a white rump that is easily seen from behind in flight.

Tail length compared to total length

	Total length	Tail length
Crested argus pheasant	240cm	173cm
Peacock	225cm	160cm
Lady Amherst's pheasant	150cm	100cm
Pheasant	80cm	35cm
Red kite	60cm	25cm
Red-billed blue magpie	40cm	23cm
Paradise whydah	38cm	26cm
Malachite sunbird	25cm	14cm
Grey wagtail	19cm	8cm
Long-tailed tit	14cm	7.5cm

*The coverts are feathers which cover the bases of the wing and tail feathers.

Beaks and feet

Unique beak

The wrybill, a New Zealand plover, is the only bird in the world with a beak that curves sideways. It uses this odd beak to probe for insects under stones on beaches, but no-one knows why it is curved.

Upside-down feeder

The flamingo holds its unusual curved beak upside down for feeding. It sweeps it through shallow water, stirring up mud. Water is sucked into the beak and then pumped out through its sieve-like edges, leaving behind tiny shrimps and algae.

Getting a good grip

Birds never fall off branches when they go to sleep. They naturally grip any branch they land on, as their feet automatically lock into position with the toes clamped around the branch. To move, birds use their toe muscles to release their grip.

Record runner

The flightless ostrich has feet with only two toes, which are the most highly adapted for running of all birds. It can easily run at about 48kph (30mph) for 15-20 minutes, and over 70kph (43mph) in short bursts.

Types of toes

Most birds have four toes, but some have three and the ostrich has only two. Perching birds have feet to grasp branches, swimmers have webbed or lobed feet, and birds of prey have large, sharp talons.

Webbed foot
Canada goose

Sharp talons
Golden eagle

Lobed toes
Red-necked grebe

Perching foot
Greenfinch

Beak facts

Longest	Australian pelican	34-47cm
Longest for its size	Sword-billed hummingbird	10cm (Total length: 20cm)
Shortest	Glossy swiftlet	3mm
Broadest	Shoebill	about 12cm
Largest for its size	Toco toucan	23cm (Total length: 66cm)

Seed-eaters

Finches, buntings, parrots and other birds that eat seeds have stout, strong beaks, often with a hooked tip. These powerful beaks are used to open tough seed casings. Crossbills have the most extreme adaptation. They use their awkward-looking beaks to force open the cones of conifer trees.

Puffins are the only birds to moult their beaks. In other birds, beaks constantly grow and wear down throughout their lives. Puffins have brightly coloured beaks for the mating season. The outer layer is then shed, leaving them with smaller, dull beaks for the rest of the year.

Lily-trotter

Jacanas have the longest toes of any bird. Those of the African jacana are up to 8cm (3in) long including the very long claws. The toes spread the bird's weight so that it can walk across floating waterweeds and lily pads in search of food without sinking.

Sensitive probes

Birds with long beaks used for probing for buried food can actually feel with their beaks. Snipes rely on their sensitive beaks when probing deep into wet mud in search of worms. Their beaks are also so flexible that the tip can be opened to grasp worms underground.

Pelicans have beaks with giant pouches of soft, elastic skin, which they use to scoop up fish from water. The pouch is so massive that it can hold several times more food than the pelican's stomach. Fully stretched underwater, it can hold about 13 litres (three gallons) of water, as much as a large bucket.

Fantastic fit

The snail kite of North and South America has a long, curved beak that fits exactly inside the shell of the apple snail on which it feeds. Its beak can cut through the muscle holding the snail in its shell.

Food and feeding

Feasting or starving

The smaller a bird is, the more time it needs to spend feeding. Big eagles can starve for several days without ill effect, but the tiny goldcrest of Europe needs to eat all day long in winter just to have enough energy to survive the nights.

Heavy hoatzin

The odd-looking hoatzin of the Amazon forests eats leaves and fruit. Its food is stored and also partly digested in an enormous crop, which weighs about one-third of its body weight. The hoatzin is a poor flier and when its huge crop is full it even has difficulty jumping from branch to branch in the trees where it lives.

Cuckoo's caterpillars

Hairy caterpillars have a mild poison in their hairs which brings people out in a rash and makes most birds that might eat them sick. But the cuckoo is able to eat this tasty treat. Every so often, the inside of the cuckoo's stomach, including the caterpillar hairs, peels away and the cuckoo coughs it up in a ball.

Vampire bird

The sharp-beaked ground finch of the Galapagos Islands is a seed-eater, but it is also known to behave like a vampire. Using its sharp beak, it pecks holes in the wings of nesting masked boobies and drinks their blood. The boobies do not seem to mind and the finches get a nourishing drink.

DID YOU KNOW?

Many birds that feed on plants swallow stones and grit to help their bodies grind down the plant material. Birds in captivity may swallow other things if they cannot find stones.

An ostrich in London Zoo was found on its death to have swallowed an incredible variety of things. These included an alarm clock, 91cm (3ft) of rope and a selection of coins.

Feeding in flight

Swifts are remarkable for spending virtually their whole lives in the air. They sleep, feed and drink on the wing. To feed, they open their wide mouths and catch flying insects. As a result, the swift's beak has become reduced to little more than a rim around its mouth.

How much food?

Bird	Average food per day	Equivalent to
Pelican	1.8kg fish	Half its body weight
Eagle	up to 1kg meat	Quarter of its weight
Giant hummingbird	15g nectar or insects	Over half its weight
Waxwing	210g berries	Three times its weight

Not a fussy feeder

The bird with the widest variety of diet ever recorded is the North American ruffed grouse. Its food is known to have included at least 518 kinds of animals and 414 different plants.

Woodpecker weapons

Woodpeckers have strong, pointed beaks to chisel into wood and sensitive, long tongues to probe for insects and grubs. The tongue may be sticky, as in the green woodpecker, or barbed and harpoon-like as in the great spotted woodpecker. A special mechanism allows it to extend over 10cm (4in) beyond the beak tip.

Hummingbirds

Hummingbirds feed on nectar, sucking it up with their long tubular tongues while they hover in front of flowers. Although they appear to be still while hovering, their wings beat at incredible speed with the tips tracing a figure of eight. Up to 80 wing beats per second have been recorded.

Gulls and golf balls

Gulls will pick up unopened shellfish and drop them from a height in an attempt to get at the tasty contents. Herring gulls have been known mistakenly to try this out on golf balls.

Buzz, buzz, buzzard

Although it is a very large bird, the honey buzzard feeds on wasps and bees. It follows them to their nests and then digs out the grubs and honeycomb wax. The buzzard has dense feathers on its face to protect it from stings.

Amazing But True

Bullfinches raid fruit orchards, eating flower buds on the fruit trees. No-one knows why, but they are very choosy. They will strip all the flowers off Conference pear trees but not touch some other varieties.

Biggest and smallest

Almighty ostrich

Biggest birds		
Group	**Biggest**	**Weight**
Swans	Mute swan	8-12kg
Herons	Goliath heron	4.3kg
Owls	Eagle owl	4kg
Crows	Raven	1.7kg
Hummingbirds	Giant hummingbird	20g

The African ostrich is the largest living bird. Males are larger than females and can be 2.7m (9ft) tall. They weigh up to 156kg (345lb), which is about 90,000 times heavier than the smallest hummingbird.

Walking on stilts

The black-winged stilt of southern Europe, Asia and central Africa has the longest legs compared to its body of any bird. In terms of size, it is rather like a slim starling walking on stilts. The stilt's legs allow it to wade in water too deep for many other birds, in search of food.

Big babies

Some birds are at their heaviest when they are very young. A wandering albatross nestling weighs up to about 16kg (35lb). It loses a lot of this when it starts to exercise its wings and is about one third lighter by the time it is able to fly properly.

Amazing But True

When ostriches are bounding along on the run, each stride they take carries them about 3.5m (11ft) forwards. Their powerful legs are by far the biggest of any bird and can be over 1.2m (4ft) long.

Heaviest flier

The world's heaviest flying birds are the kori bustards of eastern South Africa. Huge males weigh up to 18.1kg (40lb), which is about the same as a full-size television. They have a wingspan of 2.5m (8ft).

Whopper wingspan

The strong winds that blow over the world's southern oceans help keep giant albatrosses aloft for days on end, soaring around like gliders. The wandering albatross is the biggest with a huge wingspan of more than 3.5m (11ft). A recent study showed it could fly up to 960km (600 miles) a day.

Smallest birds

Group	Smallest	Weight
Hummingbirds	Bee hummingbird	1.6g
Crows	Hume's ground jay	25g
Owls	Least pygmy owl	30g
Herons	Least bittern	50g
Swans	Black-necked swan	4.5kg

Record nests

The largest nest ever recorded was built by bald eagles in Florida, USA. It measured 2.9m (9.5ft) wide and 6m (20ft) deep. It was estimated to weigh more than two tonnes, which is about the same as two army jeeps.

DID YOU KNOW?

The smallest bird in the world is the bee hummingbird of Cuba. It measures 5.7cm (2.25in) long, of which nearly half is its beak. It is smaller than many of the butterflies in the rain forest where it lives.

Egg extremes

Ostriches lay the largest eggs of any living bird. They measure about 15-20cm (6-8in) in length and weigh around 1.7kg (3.7lb). The shell is so strong that it can support the weight of a 127kg (20st) man. The smallest eggs are those laid by the vervain hummingbird. They are about 1cm (0.4in) long.

The smallest nests are built by hummingbirds. The bee hummingbird's is thimble-sized and the vervain hummingbird's is about the size of half a walnut shell.

Flightless midget

The Inaccessible Island rail, which lives on a remote island in the Atlantic, is the world's smallest flightless bird. It weighs only 34.7g (1.2oz), about the size of a newly hatched domestic chick, and has similar fluffy feathers.

Food facts

Type of bird food	Biggest bird that mainly eats that food
Seeds	Ostrich
Leaves and grass	Mute swan
Fruit	Emu
Fish	Wandering albatross
Birds	Sea eagle
Meat	Andean condor
Insects (locusts)	White stork
Worms	Curlew

Attracting a mate

Centre stage

In many grouse species males perform courtship displays at special sites called leks. Each male claims a territory there, with the most mature and strongest commanding positions in the centre where they will attract the most females. Usually about 10-15 males gather at a lek but visiting females will choose to mate only with the one or two most dominant or attractive.

Amazing But True

As many as 400 male sage grouse of North America have been known to display on a lek about the size of 24 soccer pitches. One male mated with 21 females in a morning.

Feet first

Looking rather like soldiers, blue-footed boobies display by strutting in front of each other with heads held high. The male and female both have bright blue feet which they display prominently during their courtship.

Fancy frigatebird

Some male birds have pouches on their chest or throat which they puff out in colourful displays to attract a mate. The most showy of all belongs to the male frigatebird, whose throat pouch inflates to an enormous bright red balloon.

DID YOU KNOW?

Male birds with the showiest plumage and courtship displays do not help raise their young. They may attract and mate with many females but take no part in nest building, hatching eggs or rearing the chicks. The females have dull plumage, often mottled brown, so they are camouflaged when sitting on the nest.

Dancing cranes

Pairs of cranes perform a spectacular courtship dance before mating. In Australia, the high leaps and deep bows of the athletic brolga cranes have inspired many Aboriginal dances.

Building a bower

In Australia and New Guinea the males of some species of bowerbirds build and decorate an elaborate bower to attract a mate. The satin bowerbird builds a corridor-shaped bower of twigs about 10cm (4in) wide and decorates it with blue objects such as flowers, feathers, butterfly wings and shells. It even paints the inside of the bower with blue juice from berries, using a piece of bark.

Courting grebes

Western grebes have an extraordinary and lengthy courtship dance. A pair start by facing each other on the water, then dive and reappear side by side. Rearing up on their tails with their necks held high but their heads tilted forward, they then race across the water as if on a skateboard. The courtship continues with the pair diving and surfacing with weed in their beaks. They hold this while performing a delicate dance together.

Paradise plumage

Male birds of paradise have the most fabulous feathers in brilliant colours. Some have head or tail feathers 70cm (28in) long. Others have thin tail plumes like long, curled wires. Count Raggi's bird of paradise has brilliant red, feathery plumes on his back. He hangs upside down in a tree to show himself off to best effect. Up to ten males may display in one tree.

Preening and feeding

Many birds preen each other and rub their beaks together when courting. Others use gifts of food. The male common tern is one of many birds that offers its partner food.

Courting couples

Male and female court and pair for life	Mute swan, crow, bullfinch, owls
Male and female pair up each year to breed	Storks, herons, grebes, finches
Male courts many females. Each female nests and rears her young alone	Prairie chicken, ruff, blue bird of paradise
Female courts male and lays eggs. Male is left to hatch eggs and rear young alone	Phalaropes, African jacana, dotterel

Birds' nests

Woven nests

African weaver birds make some of the most intricate nests of all. The spectacled weaver weaves a nest of strips of leaves and grass, hanging from a branch. Starting with a ring of grass, the nest is built into a ball shape, with a long, sock-like, tubular entrance hanging from one side to keep out snakes. Some weavers build entrance tunnels as long as 60cm (2ft).

DID YOU KNOW?

Birds' nest soup is made from the nests of cave swiftlets in Asia. Huge colonies of these little birds live in vast caves, making nests of saliva stuck to the roofs and walls. It takes the edible-nest swiftlet about 30 to 40 days to build its nest. Two nests are used to make one bowl of soup.

Holed-in hornbill

The red-billed hornbills of Africa make their nest in a hollow tree. They use a tactic unique to hornbills to stop snakes and monkeys stealing their eggs and chicks. With the male's help, and using mud and droppings, the female seals herself inside the nest hole. The male feeds the female through a tiny opening.

Made to measure

The European long-tailed tit makes a beautiful, dome-shaped nest of moss and lichen, lined with feathers. Up to 2,000 feathers are used in the lining. The nest is coated with lichens for camouflage and bound up with cobwebs so that it can stretch as the young birds grow inside it.

Mallee fowl mound

Mallee fowl of Australia lay their eggs in huge mounds of earth and rotting leaves built by the males. The eggs are covered over with sandy soil and kept warm by heat from the rotting vegetation, and by the sun. The male constantly tests the temperature of the mound with his beak. If it gets too hot or cold, he opens it up or piles on more leaves and soil. These compost-heap nest mounds may be up to 4.6m (15ft) in height and 10.6m (35ft) across.

Mud oven nest

Rufous ovenbirds of South America are about the size of a thrush but build a huge, round nest, about twice the size of a soccer ball. The cement-like nest is made of mud mixed with grass and hair, and may weigh up to 10kg (22lb). It has an arched entrance from which a tunnel leads to an egg chamber. Perched on a support such as a tree stump or fence post, it looks like a native mud oven, which is how the birds got their name.

Fostering and stealing

Some birds lay their eggs in other birds' nests. Some, such as the European cuckoo, use the other, often much smaller bird as a foster parent to hatch their eggs and raise their chicks. Others, such as the American bay-winged cowbird, simply steal nests. They throw out the eggs in them, then lay their own and rear their chicks.

Nest materials

Bird	Nest usually made of
Swallow	mud, saliva
Toucan	wood chips, regurgitated seeds
Hummingbird	cobwebs, moss, leaves, petals
Chaffinch	moss, lichen, feathers, hair
American robin	twigs, grass, fibre, mud
Shag	twigs, seaweed
Flamingo	mud
Waxwing	twigs, grass, pine needles, lichen
American wigeon	grass, down feathers
Kingfisher	fish bones
Mute swan	reeds, bulrushes
Eared grebe	waterweeds
Penduline tit	pussy willow down, grass
Golden palm weaver	coconut palm leaf fibres

Amazing But True

Pied wagtails built a nest behind the radiator grille of the Royal Society for the Protection of Birds' van at Sandy, England. The van continued to be used while eggs were laid and incubated. Four young were hatched and successfully fledged.

Nesting under a roof

The nest colonies of the sociable weaver in southern Africa look like huge growths in the tops of trees. Up to 300 nest chambers may be built in one colony. The birds first lay straws across a large branch to make a roof. Straw nests are then built under it, with the straws' sharp ends facing down the entrance tunnels, making it hard for baboons to reach in or small animals to enter.

Eggs and young

Keeping eggs cool

Most eggs must be kept warm, at about 35°C, in order to hatch them. But the grey gull, which nests in the hot deserts of Chile, has to cool its eggs to keep them at the right temperature. Instead of sitting on the eggs as most birds do, it stands over them, keeping them cool in the shade of its body.

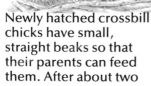

Timing it right

Blue tits lay about 12 eggs in spring. They feed their chicks on small caterpillars which hatch out to feed on new leaves just when the blue tits' eggs hatch. Because of this precise timing, blue tits have only one chance to rear chicks each year.

Little and often

Blackbirds feed their chicks on worms, which they can find all year round. They lay only four eggs, compared to the blue tit's 12, but raise an average of three broods in a season. So blackbirds can have up to 12 young, the same as blue tits, but spread them out through the summer.

Busy parent birds

Baby birds in the nest constantly demand food. A pair of great tits carried food to their chicks 10,685 times in 14 days. A female wren fed her young 1,217 times in 16 hours.

Criss cross bill

Newly hatched crossbill chicks have small, straight beaks so that their parents can feed them. After about two weeks, the upper part of the beak starts to grow and by about six weeks it bends over the lower part, forming the typical crossed bill.

Egg and chick facts

Bird	Eggs laid	Hatched after	Chicks cared for
Mallee fowl	5-35	63 days	no parent care
Mute swan	5-7	34-40 days	87 days
Emu	7-16	59-61 days	3-6 months
Wandering albatross	1	75-82 days	9-12 months
Ptarmigan	3-12	25 days	10 days
Emperor penguin	1	62-64 days	5 months
Crossbill	3-5	12-13 days	24 days
Golden-winged warbler	4-6	10-11 days	10 days

One nest of the North American redhead, a species of duck, was found to have 87 eggs. This enormous number was created by several ducks making use of the same nest, instead of each building their own. Nests where such an unmanageable number of eggs has been laid are nearly always abandoned.

Liquid diet

Newly hatched flamingo chicks have an unusual diet. They are fed on liquid produced by their parents, rather like mammals feed their young on milk. The nourishing liquid comes from the parent's crop and dribbles out of the beak as a dark, reddish colour.

Spot the chicks

Gouldian finches of tropical Australia lay their eggs in a dome-shaped, grass nest with a side entrance. Their chicks are hatched with luminous or reflective marks inside their mouths, which glow in the dark. This makes sure the parents can see them in the darkness of the nest to feed them.

Too fat to fly

Young gannets are fed so much fish that they become too fat to fly. Their parents give up feeding them when they can eat no more. They then scramble to the cliff edge and drop into the sea, where they swim off, heading south for the winter. They starve for a week or two until they are light enough to get airborne and fly the rest of their journey.

Egg recognition

No birds' eggs ever look identical. Even those in a single clutch laid by one bird will all be slightly different in colour or markings.

Guillemots lay the most varied eggs of all. They may be white, yellowish, blue or blue-green with dark lines, spots or blotches. Huge numbers lay eggs side by side on bare cliff ledges. The enormous variety helps each bird to spot its own egg when returning from a fishing trip.

DID YOU KNOW?

Baby birds have an "egg tooth" to help them break out of the shell. This is a tiny knob at the tip of the beak. Most chicks take about 30 minutes to an hour to hatch out, but chicks of large albatrosses may need six days to get out of their tough eggshell.

Sea birds

Colour-coded chicks

Kittiwakes vigorously defend their nests high up on narrow cliff ledges, chasing off any strange adult that has appeared in their absence. To make sure youngsters are not attacked by mistake, they have black on the back of their heads, which contrasts with the adults' white heads.

Porpoising penguins

Penguins are excellent swimmers. Using their wings as flippers to propel themselves along, they swim up and down through the surface of the sea like dolphins. Their top speed is about 9kph (5.5mph). They can shoot out of the water on to land or ice in one leap of up to 2m (6ft).

Foul fulmars

Fulmars belong to the group of sea birds called tube-noses, with tube-shaped nostrils on their beaks. The name fulmar may come from the word "foul", as the birds defend their nests by spitting foul-smelling oil from their stomachs at intruders.

Amazing But True

In 1979 an Aleutian tern took the wrong route and was found in England when it should have been 8,000km (5,000 miles) away in Alaska, USA. Instead of flying north to Alaska after wintering in the northern Pacific Ocean, it flew east and crossed the Atlantic Ocean.

Breeding in millions

Many sea birds find safety in numbers at breeding time. Colonies of penguins in the southern oceans contain millions of birds. Biggest of all is a colony of ten million chinstrap penguins in the South Sandwich Islands. This colony covers an area the size of 1,000 soccer pitches.

Taking the plunge

Gannets plunge-dive into the sea from heights of up to 30m (100ft) to catch fish. To help them survive the impact of the water on their bodies, they have spongy bone around the head and beak, and air sacs under the skin around the throat and breast.

Pattering petrels

Storm petrels fly low, fluttering over the sea in search of shrimps and plankton. The Wilson's storm petrel flies so close to the water its webbed feet patter along on the surface, so that it appears to be hopping or skipping along.

Penguin profiles

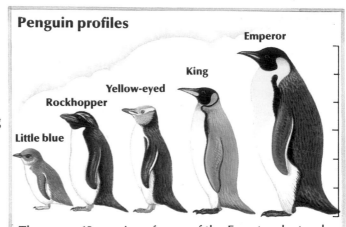

Little blue • Rockhopper • Yellow-eyed • King • Emperor

CMS
120
100
80
60
40
20
0

There are 18 species of penguins. All live south of the Equator, but only six live in Antarctica.

Pirates in the air

Skuas steal food from other ocean birds. The arctic skua catches fish and small birds, but is more likely to use its speed and flying skill to chase kittiwakes and terns, making them drop or cough up their food.

DID YOU KNOW?

Emperor penguins dive down to depths of 265m (870ft), staying under for up to nine minutes, occasionally even twice as long. Between dives, they comb their feathers to trap air in them, which helps to keep them warm in the cold water.

Swoop and scoop

Frigatebirds fly over the sea, often far from land, but never swim. They spend almost their whole lives in the air, using their enormously long wings and long, forked tail to fly with great agility. Like skuas, frigatebirds are pirates. They harass birds such as boobies, scooping up dropped food in the air with a swift downward swoop.

Gull facts

Largest	Great black-backed gull
Smallest	Little gull
Most common	Kittiwake
Rarest	Relict gull (in Siberia)
Hardiest	Ivory gull (lives in Arctic)
Longest-lived	Herring gull (44 years)
Largest colonies	Kittiwake

Water birds

Waders

There are about 200 species of wading birds, most of which feed in soft mud and sand at the water's edge. Different species can feed in the same place without competition as their beaks are adapted for finding different foods. Those with short beaks pick food from on or just below the surface. Those with longer beaks mainly probe deeper for worms and shellfish.

Beaks less than 5cm long – ringed plover, knot, sanderling, turnstone, dunlin
Beaks 5-10cm long – redshank, black-tailed godwit, oystercatcher, snipe, avocet
Beaks over 10cm long – curlew

Stained cranes

The adult sandhill crane of North America has grey plumage. But the feathers of its back, neck and breast often become coloured with rusty brown stains. Living by or near to marshes, it preens itself with a muddy beak in which there may be traces of iron, which causes brown staining.

Snake bird

The anhinga, or snake bird, gets its name from its long, snake-like neck and head, often the only part seen when it is swimming. It uses its sharp, pointed beak to spear fish, then tosses them into the air with a violent shake of its head, so it can catch and swallow them. Just like a snake swallowing food, its neck bulges as large fish pass down.

Skimming the water

Skimmers look as if they have upside-down beaks, as the lower part is longer than the upper. They fish in shallow water, flying with the lower part of the beak slicing through the water like a knife. When it touches a fish, the skimmer nods its head down and snaps its beak shut to catch it.

Amazing But True

Bright blue swans were seen on a river in the city of Norwich near the east coast of Britain in April 1990. A chemical is thought to have polluted the water but, luckily, the swans did not seem to suffer.

Whirlpool water bird

Phalaropes often spin around in circles while swimming. This creates a whirlpool, which stirs up the small animals on which they feed.

Diving from danger

Moorhens swim on ponds and lakes with their heads nodding vigorously. But if danger threatens, they dive underwater. They stay under by gripping weed with their feet and poke the tip of the beak above water to breathe.

Heron umbrella

To catch fish, the black heron crouches in water and holds its wings like an umbrella, shading the surface from the bright African sun. It may do this to see the fish more clearly, or the fish might be attracted to swim into the shade.

Sawbills

Red-breasted mergansers are sawbill ducks. They have narrow beaks with edges toothed like the blade of a saw. This gives them a firm grip on slippery fish.

Diving dipper

The dipper is the only songbird that dives underwater to feed. It stands on rocks in streams, bobbing up and down, dipping its head into the water to look for insects, worms and snails. It uses its wings to swim underwater and can even run along on the bottom.

How ducks feed

Grazers graze on grasses and other plants on salt marshes and grassy banks.	Wigeon, American wigeon
Dabblers feed on or just under the water. They can up-end, or tip up, to reach down further.	Gadwall, pintail, mallard, shoveler, teal, black duck
Divers can dive down to the water bed. They can stay under for half a minute or more.	Pochard, goldeneye, tufted duck, eider, ring-necked duck, merganser

Birds of prey

Hunters in the sky

Birds of prey are hunters, feeding on mammals, other birds, fish, insects and snakes. Owls alone hunt by night; all the others belong to a group called raptors and hunt by day. The main features of raptors are:

Excellent eyesight
Strong, hooked beaks for tearing flesh
Large feet for holding and carrying prey
Strong, sharp, hooked claws or talons for grasping prey and killing it
Powerful wings

Fire followers

Insect-eating birds of prey such as kites follow grassland fires for an easy food supply. They feed on insects that take to the air to escape from the burning grass.

Eagle eyes

Birds of prey have the best eyesight of all birds. Golden eagles, which have eyes of a similar size to ours, can see a hare from a distance of 3.2km (2 miles) in good light against a contrasting background.

Vegetarian vulture

The palm nut vulture of West Africa is the only vegetarian bird of prey. Its main food is the fruit of the oil palm tree, which it plucks from among the dense palm fronds. It also eats shellfish and fish.

DID YOU KNOW?

Like many raptors, female sparrowhawks are much bigger than males. Males catch small birds like finches and tits, while females prey on larger birds such as thrushes and pigeons. This may help them to avoid competing for food, so larger numbers can live in one area.

Raptor records

Biggest	Andean condor	12kg (3.1m wingspan)
Smallest	Philippine falconet	35g (150mm long)
Fastest	Peregrine falcon	about 100kph (level flight)
Rarest	Madagascar serpent eagle	probably less than 10 birds
Longest-lived	Andean condor	20-30 years average lifespan

Bone-breaker

One of the biggest vultures with a wingspan up to 3m (10ft) is the bearded vulture or lammergeier, also called the bone-breaker. It carries large bones from dead animals up to 80m (260ft), dropping them on to rocks to break them. It then eats the marrow and shattered bone. Lammergeiers also eat tortoises, using the same method to crack open their shells.

Ferociously fast

When hawks and falcons spot prey, they dive at great speed and hit it hard with outstretched talons, often killing it instantly. The peregrine falcon is one of the fastest, making spectacular, steep dives on to prey in mid-air at speeds of at least 180kph (112mph).

Big birds of prey		
Group	Biggest bird	Wingspan
Vultures	Andean condor	3.1m
Eagles	Wedge-tailed eagle	2.84m
Owls	Eagle owl	2m
Buzzards	Upland buzzard	1.9m
Kites	Red kite	1.8m
Harriers	Marsh harrier	1.6m
Falcons	Gyrfalcon	1.6m
Hawks	Northern goshawk	1.5m

Late start

Eleonora's falcons breed on Mediterranean islands in the autumn, long after most birds have reared their young. The chicks are hatched to coincide with the southbound migration of millions of small birds, which make easy prey for the falcon to feed to its hungry brood.

Flexible approach

The harrier hawk has double-jointed legs, which it uses in its search for eggs or chicks in tree hole nests. It clings on to the edge of a tree hole with one foot, bending its leg backwards so it can reach its other foot down into the nest.

No monkeying around

The huge harpy eagle of the South American rain forests causes terror in the treetops. It flies skilfully among the trees at up to 80kph (50mph), snatching up monkeys and sloths.

Tropical forest birds

Parrot power

Most parrots live in pairs or noisy flocks in tropical forests. They have strong, hooked beaks, which they often use in climbing. Macaws can even hang from branches by their beaks. Parrots' feet are also powerful tools and are unique in being used like hands to hold food.

Pitta patter

Pittas are colourful, plump birds with short tails and long, strong legs. Although quite able to fly, they run around on the forest floor and fly only when necessary.

Antbirds

Swarms of soldier ants marching across the forest floors in Panama are often accompanied by antbirds. The birds rarely eat the ants, but prey on the insects that are disturbed by them.

Bee my guide

The greater honeyguide of Africa is so-called because it guides honey badgers to bees' nests. The bird will call to a honey badger, or even a human, to make it follow to where it has found a bees' nest. It waits while the badger breaks open the nest to get the honey. It can then eat the grubs and beeswax.

Amazing But True

Hummingbirds drink eight times their weight in water each day. This is about a cup of water for the 20g (0.7oz) giant hummingbird. To equal this, an average-sized man would need to drink a small bath of water.

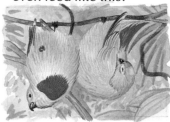

Hanging about

Sparrow-sized hanging parrots have an unusual form of camouflage. They hang upside down from a branch, bent double, and look just like leaves. They roost in this position and may even feed like this.

Parrot facts

Largest	Hyacinth macaw	100cm long
Smallest	Buff-faced pygmy parrot	8.4cm long
Rarest	Spix's macaw	under 10
Most widespread	Rose-ringed parakeet	Africa and India
Longest-lived	Sulphur-crested cockatoo	82 years (in captivity)
Country with most species	Australia	52 species

Top heavy toucan

Being 50cm (20in) long, the keel-billed toucan is a large bird, but much of this length is taken up by its huge, colourful beak. Although toucans' beaks look top heavy, they are actually hollow and very light. They are used to reach fruit from branches too small to bear the birds' weight, but why they are so huge and remarkably colourful is a mystery.

Aerial acrobats

No other bird beats the hummingbirds for aerial skills. As well as being able to hover in mid-air while they suck nectar from flowers, they can fly sideways, backwards, and even upside down. Their wings make a humming noise as they fly, which is how they got their name.

Birds to be wary of

Cassowaries are large, flightless birds of the rain forests of northern Australia and New Guinea. On their heads they have a horny casque, like a helmet, up to 15cm (6in) high. This protects them as they push through dense undergrowth. They defend themselves with powerful kicks, and are known to have killed humans with their dagger-like claws.

Preparing for paradise

The preparation made for courtship display by male birds of paradise is as elaborate as the display itself. In the forests of New Guinea, the magnificent bird of paradise clears an area about 6m (20ft) wide, even pulling leaves off trees to make sure of enough sunlight in which to show off his plumage.

Diet with a difference

Scarlet macaws in the mountain forests of South America gather on river banks and other earth cliffs to eat soil. They get vital minerals from the soil, which their diet of fruit and seeds lacks.

DID YOU KNOW?

Almost half the world's bird species are found in the tropical forests of South America. They are either breeding there or have travelled to escape the North American winter. But an area of rain forest about the size of six soccer pitches is being destroyed every minute. At this rate, most of the forests and their bird life will be gone in ten years' time.

Birds of grasslands...

Rich pickings

Vultures glide high over the African savanna for hours on end. They rarely kill prey, but fly thousands of kilometres in search of fresh carcasses. As many as 200-300 vultures may gather at a large carcass, as the birds use their keen eyesight to spot when others far away fly down to feed.

Secretary bird

The secretary bird of African grasslands is a unique bird of prey which hunts on foot. Striding about on very long legs, it hunts for small animals, including deadly poisonous snakes, which it kills by stamping on them.

Burrowing owl

The burrowing owl lives in deserted prairie dog burrows on the American plains. It hunts at night, but often stands at its burrow entrance during the day. When alarmed, it can frighten enemies by making a sound exactly like a rattlesnake.

Dry grassland birds

Typical birds of dry grasslands are:
Europe – Stone-curlew
Asia – Pallas's sandgrouse
Australia – Emu
N. America – Meadowlark
S. America – Rhea
Africa
(southern) – Kori bustard
(northern) – Temminck's courser

and deserts

Thirsty work

Sandgrouse live in deserts and fly up to 80km (50 miles) to a waterhole to drink every day. Young chicks cannot fly to reach water, so parents take it to them. They ruffle their belly feathers and soak them in water, then fly back to the nest with the water held in their feathers like a sponge which the chicks can suck. Sandgrouse may carry water like this for 30km (20 miles).

Cool colours

In deserts, colour is important for camouflage and keeping cool. The most common colouring is cream, sandy or white to blend with sand or rock. Light colours reflect heat, whereas dark ones absorb it, so pale plumage also helps birds to stay cool.

Living with little water

Deserts have less than 25cm (10in) of rain a year. Birds can live where there is so little water because they lose so little from their bodies. Their urine is much more concentrated than that of mammals and they have a higher body temperature, so they lose less water by evaporation to keep cool. In some desert birds, water loss is reduced even further by their body temperature rising during the day.

Desert fortresses

Cacti are home for some desert birds. The sharp spines keep out enemies. In America, elf owls roost and nest in holes in saguaro cacti and cactus wrens build nests in among spines of the cholla cactus.

Roadrunner

The roadrunner lives in the deserts of Texas and Mexico. Although it can fly, it usually dashes around on foot, grabbing lizards and small snakes with its beak for food.

Keeping cool

Birds have various ways of coping with high desert temperatures. Some keep cool by panting, some stand with their backs to the wind to catch cooling breezes and some go

underground in abandoned burrows or stay in the shade of rocks. Long legs help birds to keep cool, as more heat is lost from bare legs than feathered bodies. The turkey vulture even squirts excrement on to its legs and feet to cool itself.

Nocturnal birds

Batty bird

The oilbird lives in dark caves in South America. It spends its whole life in darkness, only leaving the caves at night to feed on the fruits of forest trees. Amazingly, it finds its way around in the caves by echo-location, like a bat. It makes tiny, clicking sounds and uses their echoes to tell how far it is from the walls or other oilbirds.

DID YOU KNOW?

Storm petrels spend their lives far out at sea, but have to come to land to nest. They are so weak and easy for predators to catch that they only come ashore on dark nights. Each bird finds its way to its burrow by listening to the calls of its mate and by using its very good sense of smell.

Flexi-necks

Owls have such huge eyes that there is no room to move them in their sockets. Instead, they turn their whole heads to look sideways. They have very flexible necks and can turn their heads right round to look backwards and even upside down.

Green for go

The American black skimmer sometimes feeds at night. It flies over water dragging its long beak through the surface and this stirs up luminous plankton which glow green along the skimmer's trail. Fish are attracted to the green colour, and the skimmer flies back along the same line to snatch them up.

Ear, here!

Owls' hearing is superb. Many have feathery tufts that look like ears, but in fact, their ears are large openings hidden just behind the flat discs of feathers around their eyes. The discs probably help to direct sounds into their ears. In many owls one ear is bigger than the other and one is often higher than the other. This difference makes it easier for an owl to judge exactly where a sound is coming from and so pinpoint its prey even in pitch darkness.

Sense of smell

Kiwis are unique in having nostrils at the tip of their long beaks. Most birds have nostrils at the base of the beak and use hearing and sight rather than smell to find food. But kiwis are nocturnal birds and use their sense of smell to find earthworms and insects in the dark.

Night activity

The main reasons for nocturnal activity are:
Less competition for food
Access to food not available in the day
Safety from predators for feeding or breeding

Amazing But True

The little blue or fairy penguin of southern Australia is shy at sea and nocturnal on land. But despite this, it has accustomed itself to the glare of publicity and floodlights on Phillip Island near Melbourne, the one place where it can be seen close to. Here, after dark in the breeding season, crowds gather to watch the evening parade of fairy penguins waddling hurriedly ashore to their nest burrows.

Nocturnal gull

The distinctive looking swallow-tailed gull of the Galapagos Islands is the only known nocturnal gull. Its huge eyes, for seeing squid which it catches at night, are made even more striking by crimson eyelids.

Silent flight

Unlike most other birds of prey, many owls hunt at night. To help keep their movements quiet as they swoop on to prey, their wing feathers have soft, fringed edges and they have feathers on their legs and feet.

Owl facts

Biggest	Eagle owl	71cm long (wingspan 1.5m)
Smallest	Elf owl, least pygmy owl, long-whiskered owlet	all 130cm long
Rarest	Laughing owl	probably under 10
Most widespread	Barn owl	
Strangest food	Blakiston's fish owl	crayfish
Noisiest	Pel's fishing owl	voice carries 3km
Longest-lived	Eagle owl	72 years (in captivity)

Bird voices

Variety of voices

Birds use their voices to communicate in calls and songs. Calls are simple notes, often not musical, used for a warning and to keep contact within a group. Songs are used to attract a mate and to advertise the ownership of territory. Some birds' voices have been given special names:

Bittern	boom
Diver	wail
Grebe	whinny
Oystercatcher	pipe
Nightjar	churr
Mallard (duck)	quack
Goose	honk
Owl	hoot
Dove	coo
Swift	screech

Name that tune

Many birds are named after their calls. The chiffchaff, cuckoo, curlew, kittiwake, chickadee and towhee all call their name. Some American nightjars make sounds like their names: the whip-poor-will, the poor-will and the chuck-wills-widow.

Blooming booming

In New Zealand, male kakapos make a loud booming noise to attract females, but many years they do not boom and the birds do not breed. They start to boom and nest when there is a sudden abundance of pollen on the plants that produce their favourite fruits. This tells them that there will be plenty of fruit on which to feed their chicks.

Two tunes together

A few birds, including the reed warbler, can sing two notes at the same time and so sing two tunes at once. The North American brown thrasher even manages to sing four different notes together at one point in its song. The colourful gouldian finch of Australia is equally amazing. It makes a droning sound like bagpipes while singing two songs at once.

Different dialects

Young chaffinches can sing a basic song. But they only learn a proper chaffinch song as they grow up and hear other chaffinches singing. Because they copy each other, chaffinches in any one part of Europe all sound the same, but if birds from different areas are compared, dialects or variations can be detected.

My word!

The African grey parrot is one of the most talkative cagebirds. A female called Prudle won the "Best talking parrot-like bird" title at the National Cage and Aviary Bird Show in London for 12 years from 1965-76. She could say almost 800 words, and retired unbeaten.

Amazing But True

Birds do most of their singing at dawn and dusk, but the red-eyed vireo, a small American bird like a warbler, sings all day long throughout the summer. One individual was once counted singing 22,197 times in ten hours.

Copycat birds

Marsh warblers nest in Europe but winter in Africa. They are superb mimics and can copy 60 or more bird voices. Scientists know where the birds have spent the winter because they can recognize the sounds of African birds in the marsh warblers' songs.

Barbet duet

Black-collared barbets in Africa make very loud, distinctive calls. But what sounds like a simple song is actually a duet. The first part of the call, "to", is made by one bird and the second part, "puddely", is made by its mate.

Contact calls

Migrating geese make loud, honking noises, called contact calls, to help them stay together.

DID YOU KNOW?

The familiar call of the cuckoo in Europe is made only by the male bird. Although paintings of cuckoos often show them with beaks wide open, they sing "cu-coo" with the beak closed.

Record voices

The Indian peacock has one of the loudest, most far-carrying calls which echoes for kilometres. In contrast, the notes of treecreepers are so high and hiss-like that we can hardly hear them.

A flock of long-tailed tits feeding in a wood constantly twitter to each other to keep in contact.

Instinct and learning

Bird brain or computer

Birds have very small brains compared to humans, so their ability to learn is limited. But they are born with an inbuilt ability to do many things, rather like a computer that has been programmed. This inbuilt behaviour is what we call instinct.

Nesting instinct

African weaver birds do not learn from one another how to build their intricate ball or sock-shaped nests, they instinctively know how. Scientists reared four generations of weavers in captivity without giving them any nest materials. They then gave materials to great-great-grandchildren of the original weavers and the birds built a perfect nest despite never having seen one.

Doorstep diet

Blue tits were first recorded pecking at the tops of bottles of milk on doorsteps about 70 years ago. From being inquisitive, tits learned that this was an easy source of food. The behaviour soon spread. Chaffinches, robins and song thrushes are among birds that have learnt to copy this habit.

Amazing But True

The crow family is generally thought to be the most intelligent. Many birds in the family hide food stores and have a remarkable ability to remember where they are hidden. Clark's nutcracker of North America buries pine cones and can remember 3,000 individual places where it has hidden them.

Starlings on course

In an experiment on migration, starlings were caught as they flew across the Netherlands. They were ringed and released in Switzerland. southern France, Spain and Portugal. They had instinctively flown south-west, making no allowance for having started further south

Of those recaptured later, most adults were found at their usual winter quarters near the English Channel, but the young were found in than normal. Incredibly, after returning to their breeding grounds, when autumn came again they flew back to south-west Europe for the winter.

Migration mystery

Many birds migrate over vast distances, returning to the same sites year after year. Birds are known to navigate by recognizing landmarks and by using smell and sound. They also instinctively use the sun or stars as a compass. Several species are known to have a sort of compass in their heads. But exactly how all this is used to find their way is a mystery.

Telling the time

Like many other animals, birds have an accurate sense of time. If food is put out on a bird table at the same time each day, birds quickly learn to appear at that time. This sense of time tells them when to breed and when to migrate.

Birds bathe in water or dust to help keep clean and get relief from irritating fleas and lice. Many songbirds have learnt to use ants to control lice. Formic acid from the ants is thought to kill the pests. Some birds stand on an ants' nest and fluff out their feathers so the ants run over them. Crows and jays actually hold ants in their beaks and rub them on their feathers. Crows even pick up twigs from bonfires or glowing cigarette stubs and use them in the same way.

Sophisticated fishing

Just like fishermen, the American green heron has learnt to use bait to catch fish. It picks an insect up and drops it into the water. If the bait starts to float away without luring a fish, the heron will retrieve it and even take it to a different place to try again.

Using tools

More than 30 species of birds use tools to help them get food or build nests. The woodpecker finch of the Galapagos Islands uses a cactus spine to probe into holes in wood and hook out grubs. It may use a broken spine or snap one off a cactus. It may even trim a spine to a more manageable length.

Relationships

Pecking order

Most birds live fairly solitary lives, perhaps joining up in groups to breed or to roost at night. Other birds live in a permanent flock. They have a strict "pecking order" and are ranked according to their aggressiveness. This establishes the birds' relationships to one another, so they do not fight constantly.

Easy pickings

Some birds use animals or larger birds to help them find food. African carmine bee-eaters perch on kori bustards to catch flies that flit up out of the way of the bustards' feet. North American cowbirds run among cattle to catch insects that are flushed out as the cattle graze.

Peregrine protection

Red-breasted geese nest close to peregrines in the Arctic. This strange attraction to the fierce falcons helps to protect their young. Goslings are easy prey for arctic foxes, but when the peregrines are about, the foxes stay away.

DID YOU KNOW?

Many parent birds use other birds without young to help feed their chicks. The helper may be unrelated, but is often a brother or sister of the parent, or older offspring of the pair. Red-throated bee-eaters often use helpers, which gives the young 80 per cent more chance of being reared. If helpers nest the next year, they may in turn be helped by the young they looked after.

Roosting

Birds gather for the night in huge roosts. A roost keeps them warmer, gives protection from predators, although those at the edges are vulnerable, and may help in finding food the next day. Starling roosts can contain a million or more birds, which split into much smaller flocks for feeding. A flock that has not found much to eat one day may follow one that fed well when they set out from the roost next morning.

Hoping for hornweed

Gadwalls are surface-feeding ducks. They like to eat American hornweed but cannot dive to get it. Instead they wait for coots to bring up beakfuls and then steal some or pick up dropped scraps.

Feeding together

Some birds get food by working in groups. Up to 40 white pelicans close in on a shoal of fish by forming a horseshoe around it, then dip their heads underwater together for an easy catch. Some cormorants swim in groups called rafts, diving together to catch fish in shoals.

It takes two

The turkey vulture uses its good sense of smell to detect dead animals as it flies over rain forest. But its beak is too weak to rip tough hide. The king vulture cannot smell a carcass, but has a strong beak. It follows the turkey vulture, rips the hide and both get a meal.

Biggest flocks

Passenger pigeon (extinct)	2,230,272,000
Brambling	70,000,000
Red-billed quelea	32,000,000
Sooty tern	20,000,000
Adélie penguin	2,000,000
Starling	2,000,000
Red-winged blackbird	1,000,000
Budgerigar	1,000,000
Lesser flamingo	1,000,000

Amazing But True

A male pied flycatcher will often try to pair with two females, but keeps them up to 2km (1.2 miles) apart so neither finds out about the other. If both the females lay eggs and hatch them out, the male deserts one and only feeds the chicks of the other.

Less of a look-out

Birds feeding in flocks spend less time on the look-out for predators and so have more time to feed. An ostrich feeding alone spends 35 per cent of its time looking around, but if two feed together, each wastes only 21 per cent of its time and so can spend more time feeding. Four ostriches in a group feed for 85 per cent of their time.

Chicks in a crèche

Some birds use crèches to protect chicks from predators. When eider ducklings hatch, they gather in huge crèches of 100 or more and are guarded by unrelated "aunty" eiders. This gives them much greater protection from gulls.

Birds in danger

Harming our habitats

In the past ten years, the number of threatened bird species in the world has risen sharply from 290 to 1,029. A threatened species is one in danger of dying out, or becoming extinct. Much of the increase is the result of our misuse of our environment, poisoning and destroying birds' habitats and food.

Water catastrophe

The Coto Doñana National Park in Spain is home to 125,000 geese, 10,000 flamingos and thousands of other water birds that rely on its marshland. Tourist hotels and golf courses built beside the marsh use four billion litres (880 million gallons) of water a year. Now, new developments threaten to take more than twice as much water again – a catastrophe for the birds.

Amazing But True

In 1979, the Chatham Island black robin was almost extinct, with only five birds left. A unique experiment by the New Zealand Wildlife Service, using local tom tits to foster chicks, brought the numbers over 100 in under ten years. Incredibly, every living bird is descended from a single female who lived to about 14, more than twice the normal age.

Birds as prey

Birds trapped and shot:
T Thrushes **D** Doves
W Warblers **R** Robins
L Larks **P** Birds of Prey

TDL — France
TLP
TDRW — Spain
TD — Italy
LP — Sardinia
Malta
DWP — Greece
DLP — Cyprus

Threatened birds are usually protected by law. Sadly, this does not always help them. A report in 1990 by the British-based Royal Society for the Protection of Birds claimed that millions of protected birds are being killed in Europe. Buzzards, goshawks, falcons and other birds of prey are being shot. Many other species are being trapped to sell as cagebirds or for food.

Captive breeding

Many species survive because they are bred in captivity and released back into the wild. Zoos are being asked to breed birds such as the snowy white Bali starling, which poachers have reduced to a population of 30 in its natural habitat in Indonesia.

Rare parrot

The New Zealand kakapo is a huge nocturnal parrot, too heavy to fly. Sadly, it proved easy prey for cats and rats introduced from Europe. Now, with only 43 birds left, efforts are being made to get some to breed on a cat-free island. Kakapos breed slowly, about every four years, but in 1990 one laid an egg, giving biologists hope.

Saltmarsh sparrow

Until May 1987, when the last one known died, the dusky seaside sparrow was the world's rarest bird. Its only habitat seems to have been saltmarsh in Florida, USA. Work on reclaiming part of the coast changed this marshland and contributed to the sparrow's extinction.

Some endangered birds

Imperial woodpecker	Mexico	extinct?
Paradise parrot	Australia	extinct?
Ivory-billed woodpecker	Cuba	under 10?
Bachman's warbler	Cuba	under 10?
Echo parakeet	Mauritius	under 20
Eskimo curlew	N. America	under 30?
Mauritius kestrel	Mauritius	under 30
Japanese crested ibis	China	about 40
California condor	N. America	40
Slender-billed curlew	Asia	under 100?

DID YOU KNOW?

The widespread house sparrow was at one time protected by law. It was deliberately introduced to other continents from Europe. But its spread was too successful. It bred so rapidly that by the time the law was withdrawn it had already become a pest.

Walls of death

Hundreds of thousands of birds are killed every year by fishing fleets. In the Pacific, nets up to 80km (50 miles) long, called "walls of death", are used to catch fish. They also kill shearwaters and albatrosses, which dive for food and get entangled. Similar nets in the Barents Sea kill 800,000 birds a year.

Oil pollution

Oil pollution kills huge numbers of sea birds, especially guillemots. Laws exist to stop ships deliberately pouring oil into the sea, but accidents still happen. In 1989, a huge spill from the Exxon Valdez tanker oiled 1,600km (1,000 miles) of Alaskan coast. Over 300,000 sea birds died, a record for an oil spill. 144 bald eagles and 1,016 sea otters were also killed.

Bird lifespans

Larger for longer

The larger a bird is, the longer it may live. But most birds in the wild do not die of old age, they fall victim to natural or man-made hazards. Lifespans of birds in the wild are difficult to study, but records are being built up by ringing birds. One of the problems is knowing a bird's age when it is first ringed.

Cocky cockatoo

The oldest known captive bird was a greater sulphur-crested cockatoo called Cocky, which died at London Zoo in October 1982. He was known to be over 80 years old and probably at least 82.

Albatross ages

Albatrosses are thought to be the longest-lived birds and the wandering albatross may live for about 80 years. A female royal albatross at Otago, New Zealand has been known for over 58 years and was already an adult when first ringed. As it takes 319 days to raise a single albatross chick and few survive long enough to breed, albatrosses need to live a very long time to make sure that enough chicks survive to replace them when they die.

DID YOU KNOW?

About 75 per cent of all wild birds die before they are six months old. Millions are killed by cats and a similar number by cars. Many more die from disease, starvation, bad weather and other predators such as rats, foxes and birds of prey.

Condor in captivity

Kuzya, a male Andean condor in Moscow Zoo, was at least 77 when he died in 1964. He had lived outside in an aviary at the zoo ever since being taken there as an adult in 1892.

Short and sweet

Small birds generally have very short average lifespans because most die when they are still only fledglings. Once they reach adulthood, they have a better chance of survival.

Breeding balance

Most birds produce huge numbers of young, which offset the losses they suffer. Each year, about seven million pairs of blackbirds breed in Britain and between them hatch about 70 million eggs. That would make a possible total of 84 million blackbirds by the end of the year. In reality, about 70 million fledglings and adults die and the population stays about the same.

Robins' range

European robins are short-lived, with an average life expectancy of just six months. So "the robin" that seems to appear regularly in a garden year after year is almost certainly a succession of different birds. The greatest age so far recorded for a robin in the wild is 12 years and 11 months, but this is exceptional.

Bird strikes

Some birds meet an early death when they are in collision with aeroplanes. Such accidents, known as bird strikes, cause major damage and expense to airlines and have also caused human deaths. Gulls are most often involved in bird strikes but pigeons, starlings, lapwings, cowbirds, swallows, martins, swifts and swans have all been identified.

Bird lifespans

	Average	Maximum known
Blue tit	1 year	12 years
Starling	Up to 1½ years	21 years
House sparrow	1½ years	12 years
Robin	1½ years	12 years
Great tit	1½ years	9½ years
Bee hummingbird	Up to 2 years	?
Kestrel	2 years	15 years
Woodpigeon	2½ years	16 years
Blackbird	2½ years	14½ years
Little owl	2½ years	10 years
Mute swan	3 years	21 years
Tawny owl	3¼ years	20½ years
Swift	8 years	16 years
Kiwi	10 years?	?
Emperor penguin	20 years	?
Common crane	?	50 years
Ostrich	30-40 years	68 years

Migration map

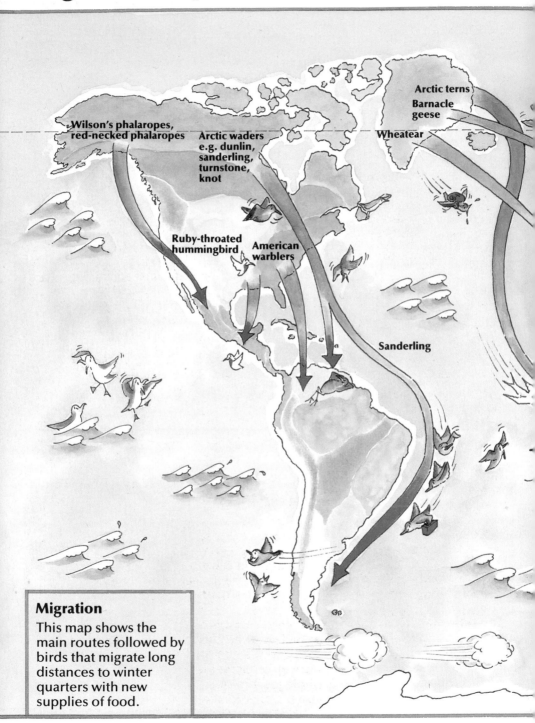

Arctic terns
Barnacle geese

Wilson's phalaropes, red-necked phalaropes

Arctic waders e.g. dunlin, sanderling, turnstone, knot

Wheatear

Ruby-throated hummingbird

American warblers

Sanderling

Migration

This map shows the main routes followed by birds that migrate long distances to winter quarters with new supplies of food.

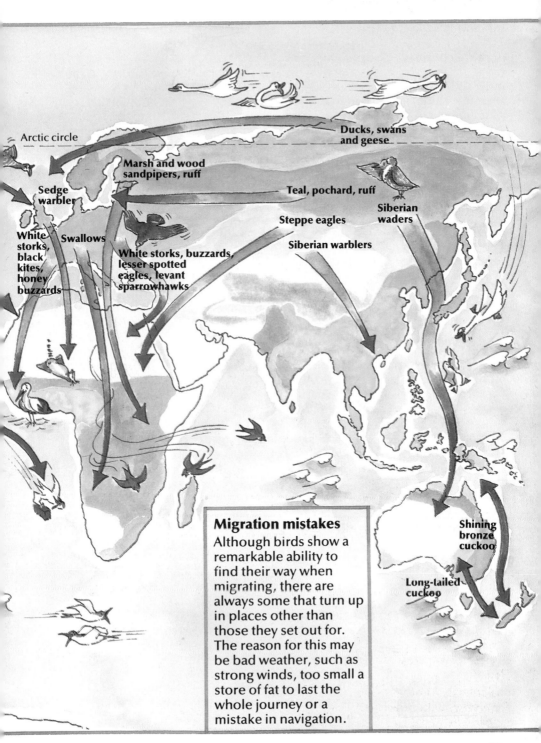

Arctic circle

Ducks, swans
and geese

Marsh and wood
sandpipers, ruff

Teal, pochard, ruff

Sedge
warbler

Siberian
waders

Steppe eagles

White
storks,
black
kites,
honey
buzzards

Swallows

White storks, buzzards,
lesser spotted
eagles, levant
sparrowhawks

Siberian warblers

Migration mistakes
Although birds show a
remarkable ability to
find their way when
migrating, there are
always some that turn up
in places other than
those they set out for.
The reason for this may
be bad weather, such as
strong winds, too small a
store of fat to last the
whole journey or a
mistake in navigation.

Shining
bronze
cuckoo

Long-tailed
cuckoo

Glossary

Bill Another word for beak.

Breeding plumage The plumage during the courtship and nesting season. In most species, only males develop specially coloured or shaped breeding plumage to attract a mate.

Breeding season The time of year, usually spring, when birds find a mate, build a nest and rear young.

Camouflage Plumage colours and patterns that blend with a bird's background and hide it from enemies.

Clutch The number of eggs a bird lays at one time.

Colony A group of birds of the same species nesting close together.

Courtship display Special behaviour to attract a mate. It may involve showing off breeding plumage or brightly coloured skin, special calls or dances.

Coverts The feathers covering the bases of the wing and tail feathers. The tail coverts grow long and showy in the breeding plumage of some birds.

Crepuscular birds Birds such as woodcock that are most active at dawn and dusk, when they hunt for food.

Crop A pouch-like part of the gullet of many birds in which food is stored and may be partly digested.

Diurnal birds Birds that are active during the day and sleep at night.

Fledgling A young bird that has just started to fly.

Flock A large group of birds moving around together.

Glide To fly with wings kept still and stretched out.

Incubate To keep an egg at the right temperature, usually about 35°C, for the chick to develop inside, until it is able to hatch out of the shell. Most birds sit on eggs to keep them warm.

Lek An area where male birds gather to display to females in the breeding season.

Length Birds are measured from the tip of the beak to the tip of the tail, as if laid out flat.

Migration Long-distance journeys made by some birds, according to the seasons, usually between their nesting area and wintering area.

Moulting The shedding of feathers, usually once or twice a year. In most birds, feathers drop out singly as new ones grow underneath.

Nestling A young chick in the nest, unable to fly or feed itself.

Nocturnal birds Birds such as most owls that are active at night, hunting for food.

Plumage A bird's covering of feathers.

Predator A bird or other animal that hunts and kills birds or animals for food.

Roost Sleep. The place where birds sleep is also called a roost. Some birds such as waders may gather in roosts numbering tens of thousands of birds.

Wingspan The measurement from one wing tip to the other when the wings are fully spread.

Index

OCEAN FACTS

Anita Ganeri

CONTENTS

Illustrated by Tony Gibson and Isabel Bowring

Designed by Tony Gibson

**Consultant: Dr David Billett,
Institute of Oceanographic Sciences,
Surrey, England**

The salty seas

Watery Earth

Over two thirds of the Earth is covered in sea water. This lies in the Pacific, Atlantic, Indian Arctic and Southern Oceans. Together they form a continuous stretch of water which covers an area nine times bigger than the Moon's surface. The oceans contain 97 per cent of all the water on the Earth.

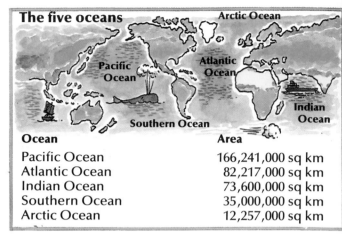

The five oceans

Ocean	Area
Pacific Ocean	166,241,000 sq km
Atlantic Ocean	82,217,000 sq km
Indian Ocean	73,600,000 sq km
Southern Ocean	35,000,000 sq km
Arctic Ocean	12,257,000 sq km

Why is the sea blue?

On sunny days the sea looks blue because it reflects the blue light rays from the Sun. The Yellow Sea near China gets its colour from yellow clay washed down by rivers. The Black Sea is coloured by mud blackened by hydrogen sulphide gas. The White Sea gets its name from the ice which covers it for 200 days each year.

DID YOU KNOW?

The Earth formed some 4,600 million years ago. Soon afterwards, the early oceans began to fill with water. Water vapour gas rose from volcanoes and hot rocks on the new Earth's surface. As it cooled, it formed storm clouds and soon the first rain fell to form the seas. The first seas were as acidic as lemon juice and only a few degrees below boiling point.

Sea water soup

Sea water contains about three per cent of sodium chloride, or common salt. This is the same as putting two cupfuls of salt in a bucket of water. It also contains many other chemicals, including magnesium, calcium and even traces of arsenic and gold. Some of the salt comes from undersea volcanoes. Most comes from the land. As rain falls, it dissolves salt in the rocks, and rivers carry it into the sea.

Oceans and seas

Ocean	Largest sea	Area in sq km
Pacific Ocean	South China Sea	2,974,600
Atlantic Ocean	Mediterranean Sea	2,505,000
Indian Ocean	Arabian Sea	7,456,000
Southern Ocean	Weddell Sea	8,000,000
Arctic Ocean	Barents Sea	1,300,000

Ocean or sea?

In some places the oceans are divided into different areas, called seas. Some seas are parts of the open ocean, such as the Sargasso Sea in the Atlantic Ocean. Other seas are partly enclosed by land, such as the South China Sea. This sea covers an area bigger than Argentina.

Amazing But True

Without sea plants, there would have been no animal life on Earth. Sea plants appeared 3,500 million years ago. They were tiny blue-green algae which gave off oxygen as they made their food. Over several million years enough oxygen collected in the atmosphere to support the first animals. Today algae produce over half of the world's oxygen.

The salty sea

The amount of salt in sea water is called its salinity. This is measured as the number of parts of salt in one thousand parts of water. It is written as ‰. In most places the salinity of the oceans is about 35‰. There is enough salt contained in the sea to cover the land with a layer 153m (520ft) thick.

Sea and sound

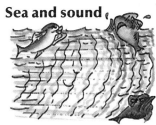

Sound travels through sea water about 4.5 times faster than it does through air. The sound of an undersea explosion off Australia reached Bermuda, half way round the world, just 144 minutes later.

Water supply

Oceans play a vital part in the world's weather. As the Sun shines on the sea, millions of litres of water rise into the air as invisible water vapour. It cools to form clouds and falls back to the Earth as rain or snow. Rivers and streams carry the water back to the sea and the water cycle starts again. Little new water is ever made on Earth. The same supply is used over and over again.

Restless oceans

Changing oceans

The Earth's hard crust is split into seven large pieces and many smaller ones, called plates. These lie like giant rafts on the layer of softer rock beneath the crust. As the plates drift apart or collide, they change the shape and size of the world's oceans.

Ancient oceans

About 170 million years ago all the continents formed one landmass called Pangaea. Around it lay a vast ocean, Panthalassa.

As Pangaea split into today's continents, the Indian, Atlantic and Southern Oceans were created. Panthalassa shrank to half its original size and became the Pacific Ocean.

Cracking up

New crust is constantly being made under the sea. As underwater plates move apart, liquid rock, called magma, rises to plug the gap. It cools and forms huge mountain ranges called spreading ridges. The ocean floor grows by about 4cm (1.5in) a year. When Christopher Columbus sailed across the Atlantic in 1492, the ocean was 20m (66ft) narrower than it is today.

Sliding under

When underwater plates collide, one plate is often pushed under the other and melts back into the Earth. These are called subduction zones. They form long, narrow trenches in the sea bed, over 10km (6 miles) deep. Without subduction zones, the Earth would have grown about a third bigger in the last 200 million years because of all the new crust made.

Fossil sea shells and slivers of ocean crust found high up on Mount Everest show that the Himalayas were once part of the sea floor. Today they are 500km (310 miles) from the sea. They formed 40 million years ago when India drifted north and crashed into Asia. This collision pushed seabed rocks 8km (5 miles) into the air.

Rock ages

Compared to the continents, the sea bed is very young indeed. The oldest continental rocks are about 3,800 million years old. The oldest pieces of ocean crust are only 180-200 million years old. They formed at the time of the early dinosaurs.

Island birth

Volcanoes are common along ocean ridges. In November 1963 an underwater volcano erupted near Iceland and formed a new island called Surtsey. Four days later Surtsey was 61m (200ft) high and 610m (2,000ft) long. Within just 18 months the first leafy green plant was growing on the island. Five years later there were 23 bird species and 22 insect species living on Surtsey.

Salt lake

About 6.5 million years ago the Mediterranean Sea became cut off from the oceans. In about 1,000 years the water dried up, leaving the sea bottom caked in a layer of salt 1km (0.6 miles) thick. Then the sea level rose in the Atlantic and water flowed back into the sea over the Straits of Gibraltar in the biggest waterfall ever. The sea took about 100 years to refill.

Sea quakes

There are about one million earthquakes a year. Many happen underwater in the "Ring of Fire" around the Pacific Ocean. The deepest seaquakes occur beneath ocean trenches, up to 750km (470 miles) below sea level. Most are never felt but in 1947 a seaquake off the Mexican coast shook a ship so violently that its cargo of heavy steel shifted 15cm (6in) along the deck.

Flood warning

Today about a tenth of the Earth is covered in ice. Scientists are worried that burning coal, oil and wood is making the Earth warmer. A rise of 4°C (7°F) would melt all the ice and raise sea level by about 70m (230ft). Coastal cities, such as Sydney, Tokyo and New York would be drowned.

Under the sea

Seascape

Under the sea, the landscape is as varied as on land. Scientists divide the sea up into different "zones", depending on the depth of the water. This profile shows the average depth of the water in each zone.

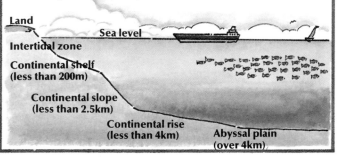

Land
Sea level
Intertidal zone
Continental shelf (less than 200m)
Continental slope (less than 2.5km)
Continental rise (less than 4km)
Abyssal plain (over 4km)

Land margins

The continental shelf, slope and rise form the continental margin around the land. The width of the continental shelf varies from about 1km (0.6 miles) on the Pacific coast of South America to 1,200km (745 miles) around northern Siberia. Most of the fish we eat come from the waters over the continental shelves.

Mountain maze

There are underwater mountains in all the oceans. Some are so huge they rise above the surface. Others, called seamounts, are volcanoes which never grow above sea level. There are about 10,000 seamounts on the ocean floor, all over 1km (0.6 miles) high. Great Meteor seamount in the Atlantic is over 100km (62 miles) wide at its base and 4km (2.5 miles) high.

DID YOU KNOW?

1
Mauna Kea

The highest mountain on Earth is not Mount Everest, but Mauna Kea in the Pacific Ocean. This volcano rises 10,203m (33,476ft) from the sea floor to form one of the Hawaiian islands. Mount Everest is the highest mountain on land, at 8,848m (29,029ft).

Under pressure

The deeper you go under the sea, the greater the pressure of the water pushing down on you. For every 10m (33ft) you go down, the pressure increases by 1.1kg per sq cm (15lb per sq in). In the deepest ocean, the pressure is equivalent to the weight of an elephant balanced on a postage stamp.

Rolling plains

Abyssal plains cover nearly half the sea floor. They are over 4km (2.5 miles) below sea level and are the flattest places on Earth. Even on their steepest slopes, you would have to walk 2km (1.2 miles) to climb just 2m (6ft).

Cold and dark

The sea gets darker and colder the deeper you go. Most sunlight is absorbed in the top 10m (33ft) of water. No light at all reaches below 1,000m (3,280ft), even on the sunniest day. The surface water may be over 21°C (70°F), but 1,500m (4,920ft) down it is as cold as the inside of a fridge.

Amazing But True

The deepest point on Earth is the Marianas Trench in the Pacific. It is 11,034m (36,200ft) deep. If a 1kg (2.2lb) steel ball were dropped into the trench, it would take over an hour to reach the bottom.

Ocean depths

Ocean	Average depth	Deepest point
Pacific	4,200m	11,034m
Atlantic	3,300m	9,560m
Indian	3,900m	9,000m
Southern	3,730m	8,264m
Arctic	1,300m	5,450m

Black smokers

Hot water seeps up through cracks in the Pacific sea floor at temperatures of over 350°C (662°F). As it reacts with minerals in the rocks the water turns black. The minerals themselves form chimney stacks as tall as houses around the cracks. The water gushes out of the chimney like black smoke.

Deep sea carpet

About three-quarters of the deep ocean floor is covered in a thick, smooth ooze. This is made up of the bodies of countless animals and plants which have drifted down from the surface, mixed with mud. The ooze collects at just 6m (20ft) every million years. It is usually 300m (948ft) thick but can be up to 10km (6.2 miles) thick.

Avalanche

Underwater earthquakes can trigger off great avalanches of mud and sand which cascade down the continental slope. These are called turbidity currents. They can cover areas of the sea bed the size of France with a layer of mud over 1m (3ft) thick. In 1929 a huge turbidity current 100km (62 miles) wide snapped apart 13 undersea telephone cables near to Newfoundland, Canada.

Oceans in motion

On the move

Ocean water is always on the move. The wind drives huge bands of water, called currents, around the world. The West Wind Drift current flows round Antarctica. It carries over 2,000 times more water than the Amazon, the largest river on Earth.

The world's main currents

Warm currents may be as hot as 30°C, while cold currents may be as chilly as –2°C.

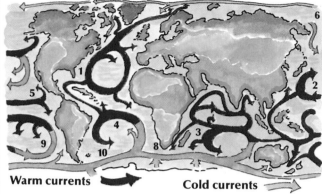

Warm currents

1 Gulf Stream
2 Kuroshio
3 Agulhas
4 South Equatorial
5 Equatorial counter

Cold currents

6 Oyashio
7 Labrador
8 Benguela
9 Humboldt (Peru)
10 West Wind Drift

DID YOU KNOW?

Currents affect the Earth's climate by driving warm water from the Equator and cold water from the Poles around the Earth. The warm Gulf Stream brings milder winter weather to Bergen, Norway than to New York, much further to the south. It keeps the Norwegian coast an incredible 24°C (43°F) warmer than other places equally far north.

Welling up

Off the coast of Peru, cold water rises up from the depths. It is very rich in nourishment and produces food for millions of fish and birds. In a single year fishermen may catch 10 million tonnes of anchovies alone. Every two to ten years, this food supply is destroyed by a warm current called El Niño.

Horse latitudes

On either side of the Equator there are calm belts of ocean with very little wind. These are called the horse latitudes because sailing ships carrying horses were often stuck in them for days. The sailors had to throw the horses overboard as they ran out of food for them.

Water attraction

Twice a day, tides make the sea level rise and fall. Tides are caused by the Moon and Sun pulling the water into giant bulges on either side of the Earth.

When the Moon and Sun pull in a straight line, they cause very high tides and very low tides. These are called spring tides.

When the Moon and Sun pull at right angles, they cause lower high tides and higher low tides. These are called neap tides. Spring and neap tides happen twice a month.

Extreme tides

The greatest tides happen in the Bay of Fundy, Canada. They can rise over 15m (50ft), high enough to drown a five-storey building.

The ground under our feet also rises and falls twice a day, just as the oceans do. When the Moon is directly overhead, it rises by 50cm (18in), three times the width of this book.

Tsunami terrors

Tsunamis are giant waves caused by earthquakes or volcanic eruptions under the sea. They speed along as fast as jet planes. As they near land they rear up to great heights and can drown whole islands. The largest tsunami known rushed past Ishigaki Island, Japan in 1971. It was an incredible 85m (278ft) high. It caused no damage but tossed a 750-tonne block of coral 2.5km (1.5 miles).

Making waves

Waves are caused by the wind blowing across the surface of the sea. The stronger the wind and the longer it blows, the bigger the waves are. Waves only disturb the surface of the water. Submarines only have to dive to about 100m (328 ft) to avoid being battered by even the severest storms.

Giant waves

The highest recorded natural wave was 34m (112ft) high. It was seen by *USS Ramapo* in 1933. Some of the biggest waves happen along the south-east coast of Africa. In June 1968, the tanker *World Glory* was broken in two by a series of waves about 30m (98ft) high.

Along the shore

Coast to coast

If all the coastlines were straightened out, they would reach to the Moon and half way back again. These are the top ten coastlines:

Country	Length
Canada	90,908km
Indonesia	54,716km
USSR	46,670km
Greenland	44,087km
Australia	25,760km
Philippines	22,540km
USA	19,924km
New Zealand	15,134km
China	14,500km
Greece	13,676km

Taking a beating

Along the coastline, the land is constantly being worn away by the force of the waves. This is called erosion. The waves carve out cliffs, caves and high arches along the shore. At Martha's Vineyard, Massachusetts, USA, the cliffs are being eaten away by 1.7m (5.5ft) a year. The lighthouse has been moved three times to prevent it slipping into the sea.

DID YOU KNOW?

The world's highest sea cliffs are on the north coast of Moloka'i, Hawaii. They are 1,005m (3,300ft) high, over three times as tall as the Eiffel Tower, Paris.

Sand colours

Sand forms when wind and rain wear down rocks into tiny pieces. Yellow sand also contains minute pieces of quartz. Pink or white sand contains coral, and green sand contains the gem, olivine. Black sand contains volcanic rock or coal.

Sticky customer

Animals living along the shore have to survive being battered by the waves. A limpet clings to its rocky perch so firmly that it would take a force 2,000 times the limpet's own weight to prise it off. Limpets feed on seaweed, using a rasping tongue with over 2,000 tiny teeth.

Slimy seaweed

Another problem faced by life on the shore is the danger of drying up when the tide goes out. Seaweeds keep moist by covering themselves with slimy mucus. The longest seaweed in the world is the Pacific giant kelp. It grows 60m (196ft) long, at an amazing 45cm (18in) a day.

Prickly character

Sea urchins sometimes disguise themselves from enemies by draping scraps of seaweed over their spines. Most sea urchins are fist-sized but some grow to 36cm (14in) across. Using their spines and sharp teeth, sea urchins burrow into sand and rock. A Californian sea urchin drilled 10mm (0.39in) into a solid steel girder. This took 20 years.

Hitching a lift

Hermit crabs borrow discarded sea-shells to protect their soft bodies. As they grow, they find a bigger house to move into. Sea anemones hitch lifts on the crab's shell and share its food. In return, they protect the crab from enemies with their stinging tentacles.

Mud and mangroves

Mangrove trees grow in huge muddy swamps where tropical rivers flow into the sea. The trees may be 40m (131ft) tall. Their long, tangled roots anchor them in the shifting mud. Saltwater can kill plants so mangroves eject waste salt through their leaves or store it in old leaves which they then shed.

Amazing But True

Mudskippers are odd fish which spend much of their time out of water in mangrove swamps. They take in oxygen through their skin. The Malayan mudskipper's fins form suckers so it can climb easily up the mangrove trees.

Riding the surf

The plough snail lives in southern Africa. When the tide is out, the snail burrows into the sand. As the tide comes in, it comes to the surface and sucks water into its foot. Using its foot like a surf-board, it lets the water sweep it high up the shore to find food.

Seashore molluscs

Molluscs are a huge group of animals found on land and in water. They range from octopus and squid to tiny seashells. These are some of the molluscs found along the shore:

Bivalves (Double shell)
Mussel
Oyster
Scallop
Razor shell

Univalves (Single shell)
Limpet
Winkle
Whelk
Cowrie

Coral

Coral builders

Huge coral reefs are built by tiny animals called polyps. They use chemicals from sea water to build hard skeletons around their soft bodies. The polyps are helped by tiny plants living inside them. Millions of polyps live in vast colonies. When they die, layers of hard coral skeletons are left. Coral grows at about the same rate as fingernails.

Longest reef

The Great Barrier Reef is the longest coral reef and the biggest structure ever built by any living creature. It stretches for 2,028km (1,260 miles) off the north-east coast of Queensland, Australia, covering an area the size of Iceland. The reef has taken at least 15 million years to grow to its great size. It is so vast that it can even be seen from the Moon.

Clamming up

Coral reefs are home to thousands of creatures. The giant clam has the largest shell in the world. It can be 1.2m (4ft) wide and weigh over 0.25 tonnes. The two halves of the shell fit together so tightly that they can grip a piece of thin wire.

Good shot

Pistol shrimps are only about 5cm (2in) long but possess deadly weapons. When a fish passes, the shrimp snaps its large right claw making a sound like a pistol shot. This sends shock waves through the water, stunning fish up to 1.8m (6ft) away. The shrimp then has time to close in for the kill.

DID YOU KNOW?

Every day coral grows a new band of limestone on its skeleton. Its rate of growth is affected by the seasons, Moon and tides. Scientists studying coral fossils have worked out that 400 million years ago, the year was 400 days long. Since then, days have been getting one second shorter every 132 years.

Sea pens

Sea pens are soft corals, related to the stony reef builders. They are named after old-fashioned quill pens because they look like feathers sticking up from the sea floor. Some would reach a person's waist, others are just a few centimetres tall. At night they glow with ripples of purple light if they are touched.

Sensitive coral

Reef-building coral is very sensitive and grows best in water with the following features:

1. **Temperature** – warm water, between 25-29°C.
2. **Depth** – water less than 25m deep.
3. **Saltiness** – water no saltier than 30-40 parts of salt to a thousand parts of water.
4. **Purity** – water must be clear and unpolluted.

Crown of thorns

Large chunks of the Great Barrier Reef are being eaten away by "crown of thorns" starfish. These strange creatures have up to 23 arms and are covered in thick, red spines.

Home, sweet home

Pencil-thin pearlfish live in the bodies of some sea cucumbers. The fish are about 15cm (6in) long. As many as three pearlfish spend the day sleeping inside one sea cucumber, with their heads sticking out of its tail end.

Sweet dreams

Parrot fish have a most ingenious way of keeping safe while they sleep. At night, they secrete a jelly-like bubble around their bodies. This sleeping bag takes about half an hour to build and to break out of.

Amazing But True

Small cleaner wrasse run beauty parlours on the coral reef. Larger fish queue up to have dead skin and parasites picked off their bodies. Even moray eels, which can grow 3m (10ft) long, stay quite still while the wrasse clean bits of leftover food from their sharp teeth.

To eat a piece of coral, the starfish grips it with its arms. Then it pushes its stomach out of its body to cover the coral and takes about three hours to digest a large piece. As few as 15 of these starfish can eat an area of coral the size of a football pitch in just 2.5 years.

Coral islands

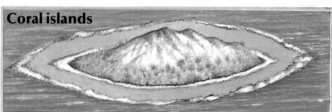

The Pacific Ocean has thousands of horseshoe-shaped coral islands, called atolls. These began thousands of years ago as coral reefs growing on the slopes of volcanic islands. As the volcano sank, the coral kept growing to form a low-lying atoll around a deep, blue lagoon.

Small fry

Mini plants

Billions of tiny plants, called phytoplankton, drift near the surface of the sea. They use sunlight and minerals from the water to make their own food. Phytoplankton start the ocean food chain. Without them, little could live in the sea. They are eaten by small sea animals which in turn are eaten by fish. Over 2 million million tonnes of plant plankton grow each year in the oceans. This is about ten times the weight of the world's population.

Part-time plankton

Sea slugs start life as animal plankton floating near the sea surface. They grow up without having to compete with adults for food and space. Some adult sea slugs are about the size of grains of sand. Others weigh over 1kg (2.2lb).

Smallest fish

The smallest known sea fish is the dwarf goby from the Indian Ocean. Adults are only about 8.9mm (0.35in) long and could easily fit on a fingernail. Another dwarf goby from Samoa is the world's lightest fish. It would take 500 adults to weigh just 1g (14,175 to 1 oz).

Seahorse slowcoach

Despite its strange shape, the seahorse is a tiny fish. Dwarf seahorses live in the Gulf Stream current, south of Bermuda. They are just 40mm (1.5in) long. Seahorses are the slowest moving fish. They hover in the water, propelling themselves along with their back fins. Even at top speed, it would take a seahorse about 2.5 days to travel 1km (0.6 miles).

Amazing But True

The staple diet of the huge blue whale are tiny shrimp-like animals called krill. Krill are only about 6cm (2.4in) long but they live in vast shoals which may be 5m (16ft) deep. A blue whale eats 4 tonnes of krill a day, sieving it from the sea water.

Blowing bubbles

The *Janthina* snail lives on the sea surface. To stay afloat it blows bubbles at the rate of one per minute and joins them together to make a raft from which it hangs upside down.

Red alert

In spring, many types of plant plankton breed quickly because of the warm weather. If a type of plankton called a dinoflagellate is involved, this growth can cause disaster.

These plants are very poisonous. They colour the sea blood red, with as many as 6,000 plants in one drop of water. They kill millions of fish and shellfish.

Long-distance travel

Sea fleas travel great distances every day. In the evening, they swim up to the surface to feed. At dawn they return to the deep sea for safety. Sea fleas are only slightly bigger than pinheads. Their 400m (1,312ft) journey is equivalent to a human being swimming 644km (400 miles) a day.

DID YOU KNOW?

Pea crabs are the smallest crabs in the world. They live and feed inside the shells of oysters, scallops and mussels. Some of these crabs have shells only 6.3mm (0.25in) long, about the size of a pea.

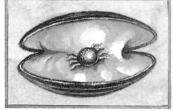

Shrinking shark

The world's smallest known shark is the spined pygmy shark from the Pacific Ocean. Adults measure just 15cm (6in) long. This is 120 times shorter than the whale shark, the world's largest shark.

More small fry

Group	Animal	Average size
Sea urchin	Sea biscuit	5.5mm wide
Starfish	Cushion star	9mm wide
Lobster	Cape lobster	10cm long
Shell	*Ammonicera rota*	0.5mm long
Squid	*Parateuthis tunicata*	12.7mm long
Octopus	*Octopus arborescens*	50mm wide
Turtle	Atlantic ridley	70cm long

Attack and defence

Man eater

The great white shark has huge jaws filled with rows of triangular, razor-sharp teeth. Each tooth may be over 7.5cm (3in) long. As the front teeth wear out, the next row moves forward to replace them. Great white sharks sometimes eat people, mistaking them for large fish. Other objects found in their stomachs include coats, a full bottle of wine and a porcupine.

A starfish can escape from an attacker by leaving some of its arms behind. All starfish can grow new arms and some species grow a whole new body from a tiny piece of arm. The process can go wrong. A starfish may end up with as many as nine arms instead of the usual five.

Deadly tentacles

The Portuguese man-of-war paralyses its prey with its long, stinging tentacles. These trail for over 30m (100ft) from its floating body. Once they have trapped some food, the tentacles can shrink to 15cm (6in) long in just a few seconds so the food can be passed to the mouth.

Puffer surprise

The death puffer fish is one of the world's most dangerous animals. Its gut, skin, liver and blood contain a poison strong enough to kill a person in just two hours. In Japan, its flesh is eaten as a great delicacy but chefs have to train for three years before they are allowed to serve it. Despite all their careful cooking, about 20 people a year still die after eating these very risky meals.

Super smell

Many fish use their excellent sense of smell to guide them to food. Sharks can smell blood from injured prey nearly 500m (1,640ft) away. A hammerhead shark's nostrils are on the ends of its hammer-shaped head. If it smells food, it swings its head from side to side to find out which direction it should swim in.

Electric shock

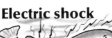

Some fish use electric shocks to kill prey and defend themselves. The most powerful electric sea fish is the black torpedo ray. It makes enough electricity to power a television set.

Hired defences

Soft-bodied Mexican dancer sea slugs combine self-defence with a good meal. They eat sea anemones, complete with their stinging cells. These cells travel through the sea slug's body and rest just under its skin. If the sea slug is touched, the borrowed stinging cells shoot into its enemy.

DID YOU KNOW?

Sea cucumbers look harmless but they have a dramatic way of fending off enemies. If a hungry fish comes too close, the sea cucumber shoots out streams of sticky threads which look like spaghetti. These entangle the attacker, giving the sea cucumber time to make a getaway.

Sinister stones

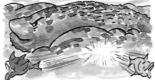

Ugly stonefish have double protection from enemies. They are well camouflaged on the sea floor, looking just like weed-covered rocks. They also have 13 sharp spines on their backs. These can pierce a rubber shoe and are deadly poisonous.

Smokescreen

Cuttlefish squirt out thick clouds of brown ink to confuse their enemies. This gives the cuttlefish time to escape. Cuttlefish ink is called sepia and was once used as artists' ink and in photography.

Sailing by

The fastest ocean hunter is the sailfish. When chasing prey, it can speed along at 109kph (68mph). This is faster than a cheetah, the fastest land animal. At high speed, the fish's sail-like back fin slots down into a groove on its back and its other fins are pressed close to its body. This makes it superbly streamlined and able to cut cleanly through the water.

More speedy sea hunters

These are the top speeds recorded for various types of fish over short distances.

Fish	Top speed
Bluefin tuna	100kph
Swordfish	90kph
Marlin	80kph
Wahoo	77kph
Yellowfin tuna	74kph
Blue shark	69kph
Flying fish	56kph
Barracuda	43kph
Mackerel	33kph

Life in the depths

Going down

Deep down in the oceans, the water is pitch black and very cold. Despite this, thousands of fish and invertebrates (animals without backbones) live in the depths there.

0 – 200m
Sunlit zone

Most sea creatures live in the top 150m where it is warm and sunny.

200 – 1,000m
Twilight zone

No plants can live below about 150m.

Below 1,000m
Deep sea zone

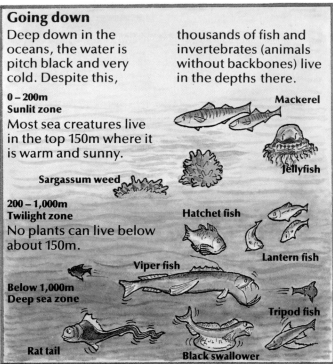

Mackerel

Jellyfish

Sargassum weed

Hatchet fish

Lantern fish

Viper fish

Tripod fish

Rat tail

Black swallower

Big mouth

Gulper eels live some 7.5km (4.5 miles) down in the Atlantic Ocean. They can grow over 1m (3ft) long. Some feed on dead animals drifting down from the surface. A tiny shrimp may take a week to fall 3km (1.8 miles) so the eels make the most of any food they find. They have huge mouths and stretchy stomachs for swallowing prey much larger than themselves.

Flashlight fish

Over half of deep-sea fish make their own lights so they can find their way in the dark. Flashlight fish have two light organs under their eyes. These are made up of billions of tiny, glowing bacteria. If danger threatens, the fish can switch its lights off by covering them with a curtain of skin.

Angling for food

Deep-sea angler fish use their lights to trap food. A long, thin fin like a fishing rod grows over the angler's head. It has a bulb of glowing bacteria dangling on the end, which acts like bait. Small fish mistake the light for a tasty meal and swim straight into the angler's mouth.

DID YOU KNOW?

Deep-sea prawns are often bright red for camouflage. The colour red is difficult to see in deep water and many deep-sea fish are colour blind and cannot see red. One fish, though, has eyes that can pick up red. It also shines its own red light to hunt for the prawns.

Deepest fish

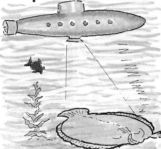

The deepest fish so far discovered may have been a flatfish like a sole. The fish was about 30cm (1ft) long and was seen 10,911m (35,800ft) down in the Pacific.

Finding a mate

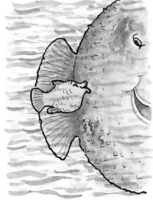

Finding a mate is difficult in the dark depths. When two angler fish meet, they make sure they stay in touch. The male weighs about half a million times less than the female. He attaches himself to her with his teeth and their bodies merge together. All that is left of the male is a small pouch on the female's side which fertilizes her eggs.

Amazing But True

One type of deep-sea squid is born with both eyes the same size. As it gets older, though, its right eye grows up to four times bigger than its left eye. Some scientists think the squid uses its large eye to see in deep water and the smaller eye to see in shallow water. Other scientists think that the opposite may be true.

Hatchet fish

The hatchet fish's upturned eyes act like binoculars to scan the water above for food. It sees small fish as dark silhouettes against the light coming from above. Its mouth is also turned up to catch food as it drifts down. The hatchet fish's body is flattened from side to side. This prevents it making a silhouette which might attract hungry predators from deeper down.

Deep-sea records

The depths below are the maximum at which each creature has so far been found. The deepest scuba dive by a human being is only 133m (436ft).

Animal	Greatest depth known
Prawn	6,373m
Sea urchin	7,340m
Sea spider	7,370m
Barnacle	7,880m
Sponge	9,990m
Sea star	9,990m
Sea snail	10,687m
Sea anemone	10,730m
Sea cucumber	10,730m

Ocean mammals

Life in the sea

Until about 65 million years ago, the ancestors of whales and dolphins lived on land. They returned to the sea to find food. Here are some of the ways they adapted to the water:

1 Bodies became streamlined for swimming.
2 Front legs became flippers.
3 Back legs disappeared altogether.
4 Nostrils became a blow-hole on top of the head.
5 Hair was replaced by a thick, warm layer of fat, called blubber, under the skin.

Snow white

Pure white beluga whales live in the Arctic Ocean. New-born belugas are reddish brown. They turn grey and finally white when they are five years old. Belugas are nicknamed "sea canaries" because they often make loud chirping noises.

Baby blue

Blue whales have the biggest babies of any animal. A new-born whale can weigh over 5 tonnes, some 1,000 times heavier than a new-born human baby. It drinks 600 litres (132 gallons) of its mother's milk a day and by the age of seven months weighs 23 tonnes. In this time its mother loses 30 tonnes.

Humpback trap

A humpback whale may trap its food by blowing bubbles. A whale circles a shoal of fish and blows a great net of bubbles around them. This confuses and traps the fish. Then the whale swims up through the bubbles, mouth open, gulping the fish down.

Amazing But True

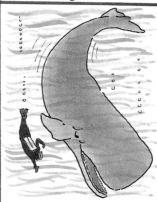

Sperm whales can hold their breath for almost two hours when they dive for food. One whale was found with two deep sea sharks in its stomach. It must have dived 3,000m (10,000ft) down to catch them.

Record breaker

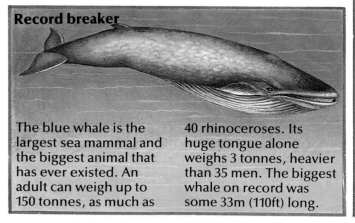

The blue whale is the largest sea mammal and the biggest animal that has ever existed. An adult can weigh up to 150 tonnes, as much as 40 rhinoceroses. Its huge tongue alone weighs 3 tonnes, heavier than 35 men. The biggest whale on record was some 33m (110ft) long.

Sea mammal diets

Mammal	Food	Daily amount
Blue whale	Krill, shrimps	4 tonnes
Sperm whale	Squid, sharks	1 tonne
Elephant seal	Squid, fish	200kg
Killer whale	Seals, birds, sharks	45kg
Bottlenose dolphin	Fish, eels, hermit crabs	8-15kg

Dolphin detection

Dolphins use sound to navigate and find food underwater. They give out high pitched clicks, about 14 times higher than human ears can hear. If the sounds hit solid objects in the water, they send back echoes. From these, the dolphin can tell where and what an object is.

Sea elephant

Seals, sea-lions and walruses belong to a group of sea mammals called pinnipedes. The biggest pinnipede is the huge southern elephant seal. The largest on record was 6.5m (21ft 4in) long and weighed 4 tonnes. It could have towered up to 3m (10ft) in height.

DID YOU KNOW?

A walrus has about 700 hairs on its snout. Each hair is about 3mm (0.1in) thick, some 40 times thicker than human hair. The walrus uses its whiskers to feel its way underwater and find shellfish to eat. It eats these by sucking them out of their shells.

Mermaid myth

Dugongs, or sea cows, may have started the mermaid legend. The largest dugongs were Stellar's sea cows. They were discovered in 1741 but sailors ate so many that the sea cows became extinct just 27 years later.

Speedy seals

The fastest seal is the Californian sea-lion. It can speed through the water at 40kph (25mph). Leopard seals are also very fast swimmers when chasing penguins to eat. To get on to land, they build up speed and shoot 2m (6ft) out of the water to land with a thump on the ice.

Birds of the sea

Walking on water

The sparrow-sized Wilson's storm petrel is one of the smallest sea birds. As it flutters above the sea looking for plankton to eat, it pats the surface of the water with its feet. This makes it look as if it is walking on the water.

Head over heels

Sea eagles perform very unusual courtship displays. In the air, the male dives down towards the female. She turns upside-down and the two birds lock their talons together. They then drop down towards the sea or land, turning cartwheels in mid-air.

Salt hazard

Sea birds take in large amounts of salty sea water as they feed. Too much salt kills birds so they have to get rid of some of it. Special glands in their heads extract salt from the water. It trickles out of the birds' nostrils back into the sea.

Spitting with rage

To drive intruders away from their nests, fulmars spit at them. The spit is made inside the birds' bodies from the plankton they eat. It is oily and smelly. Fulmars can spit very accurately and hit targets up to a metre away.

Amazing But True

Sea birds such as skuas and gulls have a special way of protecting their eyes from the glare of the sea and sky. Their small eyes contain tiny droplets of reddish oil. These work just like sunglasses to block out the harsh sunlight.

Record journey

Many sea birds make long journeys between their feeding and breeding grounds. The Arctic tern makes the longest trip of all. Each year it flies from the Arctic to the Antarctic and back again. This is a round trip of over 40,200km (25,000 miles). In its lifetime, a tern flies the same distance as a return trip to the Moon.

Sea wanderer

The wandering albatross has the longest wings of any living bird. They can measure over 3.5m (11.5ft) from one wing tip to the other. The albatross glides on air currents across the Southern Ocean. If the winds are right, an albatross may fly 900km (1,450 miles) in a day.

Express post

The magnificent frigate bird is the fastest sea bird. It can fly at the same speed as a fast car, over 150kph (93mph). On some South Sea islands, people have trained frigate birds to carry messages to other islands. The birds then return to special posts set up on the beaches.

DID YOU KNOW?

Guillemots live in huge, crowded colonies of over 140,000 birds. They do not build nests but lay their eggs on narrow cliff ledges. The eggs are perfectly designed so they do not fall off. They are long and pear-shaped with pointed ends. If the eggs are knocked, they roll in a circle and stay put.

Baby sitting

Despite temperatures of −62°C (−80°F) emperor penguins nest on the Antarctic ice in the middle of winter. The female lays a single egg, then swims off. The male is left behind to look after the egg. He balances it on his feet and spends about nine weeks without moving or eating. The female returns to feed the chick when it hatches.

Penguin facts

Largest	Emperor penguin	115cm tall
Smallest	Little blue	40cm tall
Fastest swimmer	Gentoo	36kph
Deepest diver	Emperor penguin	265m
Most common	Macaroni penguin	over 16 million
Most northerly	Galapagos penguin	Galapagos Islands

Ocean giants

Super fish

The huge whale shark is the biggest fish in the world. It grows over 18m (59ft) long and weighs 20 tonnes, as much as five rhinos. The whale shark also has the thickest skin of any animal. It is like tough rubber, 10cm (4in) thick. Despite its size, this giant fish only eats tiny sea animals and is quite harmless.

Longest bony fish

Sharks and rays have skeletons of gristly cartilage, rather than bone. Other fish have bony skeletons. The oarfish is the longest bony fish of all. It can grow over 15m (50ft) in length, longer than five table tennis tables laid end to end.

Squid records

Giant squid are the world's largest known invertebrates. The heaviest giant squid on record was found in Thimble Tickle Bay, Canada, in 1878. It weighed 2 tonnes and was about 15m (50ft) long. Giant squid have the biggest eyes of any animal. The Thimble Tickle squid had eyes 40cm (15.5in) across, nearly 17 times wider than human eyes.

Amazing But True

The ocean sunfish is the biggest bony fish. An adult is about the size of a small truck, over 3m (10ft) long and weighing over 2 tonnes. This enormous fish starts life as a tiny egg the size of a pinhead. A new-born ocean sunfish has to grow 1,200 times longer to reach the size of an adult.

The biggest crab

Crabs, lobsters and shrimps belong to a group of animals called crustaceans. Japanese spider crabs are the largest crustaceans known. The biggest spider crab ever found measured 3.7m (12ft 1.5in) across its front claws. A hippo would fit between them.

Mighty manta

Diamond-shaped manta rays are the largest type of ray. They can weigh over 2 tonnes and measure 8m (26ft) from the tip of one wing-like fin to the tip of the other. The rays swim through the water by flapping their wings. They can also jump out of the water, leaping 2m (6ft) into the air.

DID YOU KNOW?

The Portuguese man-of-war belongs to a group of jelly-like animals called siphonophores. Its tentacles can trail for over 30m (98ft). This giant is made up of as many as 100,000 tiny individual animals stuck together. Each has its own special job. Some sting or catch food. Others make the siphonophore float or pull it through the water.

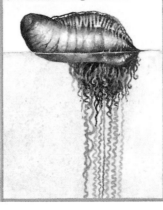

Prize pearl

Clams and oysters sometimes get irritating parasites inside their shells. They cover them with layers of the chemical, calcium carbonate, to form pearls. The biggest pearl ever found came from a giant clam in the Philippines and is called the Pearl of Lao-tze. It weighs over 6kg (14lb) and is shaped like a human brain.

More ocean giants

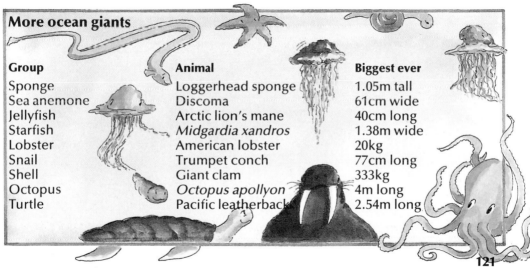

Group	Animal	Biggest ever
Sponge	Loggerhead sponge	1.05m tall
Sea anemone	Discoma	61cm wide
Jellyfish	Arctic lion's mane	40cm long
Starfish	*Midgardia xandros*	1.38m wide
Lobster	American lobster	20kg
Snail	Trumpet conch	77cm long
Shell	Giant clam	333kg
Octopus	*Octopus apollyon*	4m long
Turtle	Pacific leatherback	2.54m long

The Pacific Ocean

Vital statistics

Area: 166,241,000 sq km
Widest point: 17,700km
Length: 11,000km
Average depth: 4,200m
Maximum depth:
  11,524m
Volume:
  723,700,000 cu km

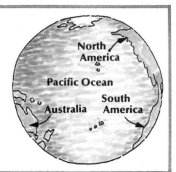

North America
Pacific Ocean
Australia
South America

Record breaker

The Pacific is the largest ocean, covering about one third of the Earth. It is over seven times bigger than the USSR, the world's largest country. At its widest point between Panama and Malaysia, the Pacific stretches nearly halfway round the world.

Epic voyages

The first people to explore the Pacific were Polynesian sailors over 2,000 years ago. They were expert sailors, navigating by the wind, waves, Sun and stars. They used stick charts to teach young sailors how to find islands by understanding the wave patterns around them.

DID YOU KNOW?

Grey whales spend the summer feeding in the Arctic. Then they swim south along the Pacific coast to breed near Mexico, returning north in the spring. This is a round trip of 20,000km (12,500 miles), about the same distance as from London, England to Auckland, New Zealand.

Land bridge

The Bering Strait separates the USA and USSR by just 85km (53 miles). This is the narrowest part of the Pacific Ocean. During the last Ice Age, the sea level was lower than it is today and the Bering Strait was dry land. The first people to live in North America crossed over this land bridge from Asia about 30,000 years ago.

Sound asleep

Sea otters live on the Pacific coast of North America, among the beds of giant seaweed. They spend most of their lives at sea and even sleep in the water, lying on their backs. They wind strands of seaweed round their bodies to stop them drifting away and sometimes cover their eyes with their front paws.

Mountain maker

In the deep ocean trenches at the edges of the Pacific, the sea bed is being dragged back into the Earth. Along the coast of Chile, the Pacific Ocean floor is being forced down under the land. This process formed the Andes mountains about 80 million years ago.

Sea serpents

There are about 50 species of sea snake, ranging from 1m (3ft) to 3m (10ft) in length. All of them use poison to kill fish for food. One drop of sea snake venom can kill three adult people. The marine cobra of the Pacific is one of the world's most poisonous snakes. Its venom is about 50 times stronger than that of a king cobra, the world's largest poisonous snake.

Amazing But True

About 2,400m (8,000ft) down in the Pacific, hot water gushes up through cracks, or vents, in the sea bed. The water is heated to 350°C (660°F) yet the vents are home to some incredible animals. Clumps of giant tube worms, each 3m (10ft) long, huge crabs and shrimps live on the vent walls. They eat bacteria which feed on chemicals dissolved in the water.

Tropical islands

The Pacific is dotted with islands. Over 100 ancient volcanoes make up the Hawaiian islands, forming a chain 2,800km (1,740 miles) long. Hawaii itself is made up of two huge volcanoes – Mauna Loa and Mauna Kea. Mauna Loa is the world's largest active volcano. It once erupted non stop for 18 months.

Galapagos giants

The Galapagos Islands lie about 1,000km (650 miles) west of Ecuador. They are famous for their unusual animals, including large marine iguanas, the only lizards that live mainly in the sea. The islands are also home to giant tortoises which can live for 200 years, longer than any other animal.

The Atlantic Ocean

Vital statistics
Area: 82,217,000 sq km
Widest point: 9,600km
Average depth: 3,300m
Maximum depth:
  9,560m
Volume:
  321,930,000 cu km
Age: about 150 million
  years

Still growing
The Atlantic is the second largest ocean, covering about one fifth of the Earth. Each year, the Atlantic grows about 4cm (1.5in) wider, pushing Europe and North America further apart. In a million years' time, the ocean will be about 40km (25 miles) wider than it is today.

Single file

Each year thousands of American spiny lobsters migrate over 100km (62 miles) along the Atlantic coast of Florida. Groups of about 50 lobsters march in single file, hooking their front claws round the lobster in front. The lobsters scuttle over the sea bed as fast as a human being can swim.

DID YOU KNOW?

Bouvet Island in the South Atlantic is the world's most isolated island. It is 1,700km (1,050 miles) away from the east coast of Antarctica. The most remote, inhabited island is Tristan da Cunha in the South Atlantic. The islanders' closest neighbours live on St Helena, some 2,120km (1,320 miles) away.

Living fossil
Horseshoe crabs live along the Atlantic coast of North America. They are not real crabs but are related to spiders and scorpions. Every spring at full moon, thousands of horseshoe crabs come ashore to lay their eggs. The eggs hatch into young crabs just in time to be carried out to sea by high tides at the next full moon.

Mountain high

The largest mountain range in the world runs down the middle of the Atlantic Ocean. The

Mid-Atlantic Ridge is over 11,265km (7,000 miles) long and 1,600km (1,000 miles) wide at its widest point. These mountains lie about 2.5km (1.5 miles) underwater and rise up to 4km (2.5 miles) from the sea bed.

Unsalty sea

For 180km (112 miles) off the coast of Brazil the water in the Atlantic Ocean is hardly salty at all. This is because of the huge amount of water poured into the ocean by the mighty Amazon River. It carries over half of all the fresh water on Earth.

Waterspouts

Waterspouts are common in the Gulf of Mexico. They form when tornadoes or whirlwinds pass from land out to sea. Winds blowing at up to 965kph (600mph) whip the sea into clouds of spray. Waterspouts may be 10m (30ft) thick and 120m (394ft) high. They look like solid water but are mainly water vapour.

Amazing But True

Each year both European and North American eels swim from their river homes to the Sargasso Sea to breed. Then the adults die and the young eels begin an incredible journey home. European eels are only about 8cm (3in) long but they swim 6,000km (3,730 miles) to the rivers. The journey takes about three years.

Methane mussels

Scientists in the Gulf of Mexico have found huge beds of mussels which live on a gas called methane. The gas bubbles out of oily sediment some 3,000m (10,000ft) down in the water. It is turned into energy for the mussels by bacteria living inside their bodies. In some places the mussel blankets are 1.8m (6ft) wide and 7m (22ft) long.

Still waters

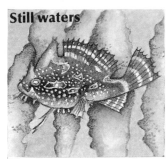

The Sargasso Sea in the North Atlantic is an area of calm water larger than India. Huge rafts of seaweed float on the surface, sheltering some unique animals. The Sargassum fish looks like a piece of the yellowy-green weed. It grips the weed with its front fins as it searches for prey.

Turtle tour

Atlantic green turtles leave their feeding grounds in Brazil and swim 2,000km (1,240 miles) to lay their eggs on Ascension Island. No one knows how they find this tiny island in the middle of the huge Atlantic. They may navigate by the stars or by smell. On the return journey the turtles and their babies hitch a lift on a current running past the island on its way from Africa.

The Indian Ocean

Vital statistics

Area: 73,600,000 sq km
Widest point: 9,600km
Average depth: 3,900m
Maximum depth:
  9,000m
Volume:
  292,131,000 cu km

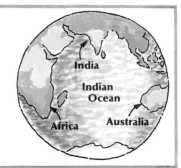

In third place

The Indian Ocean is the third largest ocean. Its seas hold the record for the warmest and saltiest water. In the Persian Gulf the sea surface temperature reaches an amazing 35.6°C (96°F) in summer. The Red Sea has the saltiest sea water in the world. It is the equivalent to two level teaspoons of salt dissolved in 0.5 litres (1 pint) of water.

DID YOU KNOW?

At night the surface of the Indian Ocean sparkles with light. The light is made by tiny sea plants called dinoflagellates. Large numbers of the plants give off enough light to read by. The lights sometimes form a wheel shape which may be up to 1.5km (1 mile) wide.

Shell shocked

The Indian Ocean is home to the world's most dangerous mollusc. The cone shell is equipped with a deadly weapon. The snail inside has a trunk-like tube loaded with poison which it injects into its victim. The snail uses poison to kill its prey of worms and fish. It can also kill humans.

Hot brines

The Red Sea floor is covered in pools of hot, heavy, very salty water called brine. These form when water trickles through cracks in the sea floor, dissolving salt and metals from the rocks. The water is heated deep inside the Earth and forced up again as brine. As it cools, the brine deposits its metal load on the sea bed.

Pearly nautilus

The pearly nautilus lives deep down in the Indian Ocean. Its shell is 25cm (10in) wide and is divided into about 40 chambers. The animal itself lives in the largest, newest chamber. By regulating the amount of fluid and gas in the other chambers, the nautilus can make itself float or sink and swim along.

Flying fish

To escape from enemies, flying fish shoot out of the water at speeds of up to 32kph (20mph). Then they glide over the surface using their tails as propellers and their fins as wings. After about 40m (130ft) they bounce back on to the surface to give them extra lift. The fish can glide for 400m (1,300ft).

Amazing But True

In 1938 scientists caught an odd-looking fish near the Comoro Islands off Madagascar. To their amazement it was a coelacanth, thought to have become extinct 70 million years ago. They later found that the local fishermen had been catching these fish for many years and using their strong, rough scales as sandpaper.

Big bang

In 1883 a huge eruption blew up two thirds of the volcanic island of Krakatoa in the eastern Indian Ocean. The sound was the loudest ever recorded. It could be heard in Australia over 4,800km (3,000 miles) away. The shock of the eruption was felt 14,500km (9,000 miles) away and caused a huge tidal wave to sweep over Java and Sumatra. The wave killed 36,000 people and carried boats 3km (2 miles) inland, leaving them stranded on top of a hill.

Deep sea fans

The Ganges and Indus carry more sediment (mud and rocks) into the sea than any other rivers. As their water pours into the Indian Ocean, the sediment sinks to the bottom and forms layers hundreds of metres thick. Undersea avalanches carry the sediment downhill where it spreads into a fan shape. The Bengal Fan is so large that it stretches halfway down the Indian Ocean.

Current changes

Most ocean currents flow in one direction all the time. In the northern Indian Ocean, though, they change direction twice a year, driven by the monsoon winds. From November to March the currents are blown towards Africa by the cool, dry north-east monsoon winds. In May the winds blow in the opposite direction, driving the water towards India.

The Polar Oceans

Arctic statistics
Area: 12,257,000 sq km
Area of ice:
　10,000,000 sq km
Average depth: 1,300m
Maximum depth:
　5,450m
**Average thickness of
　ice:** 3-3.5m
Volume:
　13,702,000 cu km

The frozen ocean
The Arctic Ocean is the smallest and shallowest ocean. It is almost entirely surrounded by land. The Arctic Ocean is frozen over for most of the year with the North Pole at the centre of a massive, floating raft of ice. In places, the ice is over 1.5km (1 mile) thick in winter.

Iced water

Fresh water freezes at 0°C (32°F) but sea water freezes at about –2°C (28.4°F) because of the salt in it. When sea water freezes, though, the ice contains very little salt because only the water part freezes. It can be melted down to use as drinking water.

Drifting off
The Arctic gets its name from the Greek word *arktos*, meaning "bear". It is home to huge polar bears which can weigh over a tonne and stand 2.4m (7.75ft) high, twice as big as a tiger. Some bears drift for hundreds of kilometres out to sea on ice rafts. Some never step on land in their whole lives.

DID YOU KNOW?

There are no penguins in the Arctic. Penguins are only found south of the equator. The two species living in Antarctica are well suited to the cold. Their feathers form windproof, waterproof coats which are so warm that the penguins can get too hot. Then they ruffle their feathers and hold out their flippers to cool down.

Whale horn

Narwhals in the Arctic Ocean belong to the whale family but have a special feature which none of their relations share. They have only two teeth, growing from their upper lip. In male narwhals, one tooth grows in a spiral, up to 2.5m (9ft) long. At mating time, males may joust with their tusks to fight off rivals.

128

The Southern Ocean

The Southern Ocean is made up of the seas around Antarctica. In winter an area of ocean twice the size of Canada is completely covered in ice. The most southerly part of the ocean is just 490km (305 miles) from the South Pole itself, at the end of the Robert Scott glacier.

Seal survival

The Weddell seal lives in the frozen Southern Ocean, further south than any other mammal. It has to dive over 300m (1,000ft) under the ice in search of food. The seal can stay underwater for up to 15 minutes but it has to surface regularly to breathe. Then it gnaws air holes in the ice with its large front teeth.

Midnight Sun

In June and July the North Pole has constant daylight. At the same time the South Pole has 24-hour darkness. In December and January it is the South Pole's turn for the "midnight Sun" and the North Pole is freezing and dark. This happens because the Poles take turns to face the Sun as the Earth travels round it.

Amazing But True

Some cod-like Antarctic fish have a special way of surviving in the icy seas. Their blood contains a chemical which acts as a natural anti-freeze. Cold can kill fish by freezing their blood or causing ice to form in their cells. The anti-freeze chemical keeps the fish's blood liquid even if the water is several degrees below freezing point.

Iced soup

Despite the cold, the Southern Ocean teems with life. In summer the water nourishes a huge amount of plant plankton which is eaten by small animals, such as krill. In turn the krill is eaten by seals, whales and birds. Krill form swarms so vast they can be seen from satellites. The largest swarm was thought to weigh about 10 million tonnes.

Ice mountains

The Arctic and Southern Oceans are littered with icebergs. These break off the ends of glaciers or ice sheets. Up to 15,000 new icebergs appear each year in the Arctic Ocean alone. The largest iceberg ever was was seen off the coast of Antarctica in 1956. It measured 31,000 sq km (12,000 sq miles), an area larger than Belgium.

Exploring the seas

Studying the sea

The study of the oceans is called oceanography. It is a mixture of biology, chemistry, physics, geology and also meteorology. In 1872 *HMS Challenger* set out on the first scientific voyage round the world. The expedition lasted for just over three years and discovered over 4,000 new species of ocean plants and animals.

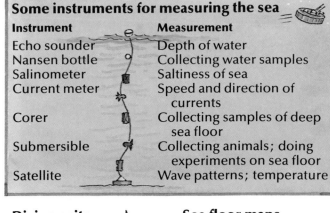

Some instruments for measuring the sea

Instrument	Measurement
Echo sounder	Depth of water
Nansen bottle	Collecting water samples
Salinometer	Saltiness of sea
Current meter	Speed and direction of currents
Corer	Collecting samples of deep sea floor
Submersible	Collecting animals; doing experiments on sea floor
Satellite	Wave patterns; temperature

DID YOU KNOW?

If divers surface too quickly after a dive, they may suffer from the "bends". Their air supply contains nitrogen gas which dissolves in the blood. If divers rise too fast, the nitrogen forms bubbles in their blood, causing very sharp pains and even death. The bends may not happen until as many as 18 days after a dive.

Diving suits

Some modern diving suits have their own built-in air supply which can last up to three days. One type, called WASP, has metal hands which are agile enough to do a jig-saw puzzle. In the past divers wore suits weighted down with lead, lead boots and copper helmets. Air was pumped from a ship.

Sea floor maps

Until very recently, scientists had little idea what the deep sea floor looked like. Today they have instruments which use sound to make maps of deep sea features, such as trenches and mountains. The instruments are towed above the sea bed, charting areas of floor 60km (32 miles) wide.

Diving records

Type of dive	Greatest depth
Breath held	105m
Scuba (breathing air)	134m
Helmeted dive	166m
Scuba (breathing gas mixture)	520m
Submersible	10,916m

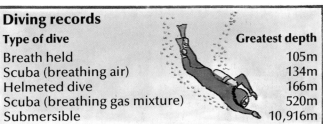

Record breakers

In 1958 the American nuclear submarine, *Nautilus,* travelled under the ice across the Arctic Ocean, a distance of 2,945km (1,830 miles). It was the first vessel ever to reach the North Pole. In 1960 the nuclear submarine, *Triton,* became the first vessel to travel round the world underwater.

Ocean expeditions

From the 15th to 18th centuries, many great explorers set out to discover new routes across the oceans. The map shows some of the most famous voyages of that time.

→ Columbus (1492-1493)

→ Vasco da Gama (1497-1499)

→ Ferdinand Magellan (1519-1522)

→ Francis Drake (1577-1580)

→ William Barents (1594-1596)

→ James Cook (1768-1780)

Amazing But True

On 23 January 1960 the bathyscaphe, *Trieste,* dived 10,916m (35,813ft), almost to the bottom of the Marianas Trench in the Pacific Ocean. The descent took 4 hours and 48 minutes. The crew travelled in a steel ball with walls nearly 13cm (5in) thick. This was to stop them being crushed by the huge pressure of the water.

Discovering Asia?

When Columbus landed in America in 1492, he thought he was in Asia. At that time people thought the Earth was a third smaller than it really is. No one could convince Columbus that he was wrong. On his second voyage in 1494 he even made his crew swear that the coast of Cuba was Asia.

Viking voyagers

The Vikings may have been the first Europeans to discover America. In about 986 AD, Eric the Red led an expedition to Greenland and founded a settlement there. About four years later his son, Leif the Lucky, is thought to have sailed from Greenland across the Atlantic to land in North America.

Ocean transport

The first boats

The first boats were made by hollowing out tree trunks with fire or a sharp tool. This is why they are called "dug outs". The earliest surviving boat is a dug-out pine canoe. It was found in Holland and is about 8,500 years old.

Sailing ships

The Ancient Egyptians were the first people to use sails 5,000 years ago. These first sails were square and made of reeds. In 1980 a new type of sailing ship was launched. The *Shin Aitoku Maru* has two square, metal sails. A computer works out when to unfurl the sails to catch the wind.

Giant ships

Modern oil tankers are the largest ships ever built. The *Seawise Giant* is one of the biggest tankers of all. Fully loaded it weighs an amazing 574,000 tonnes and is as long as 15 tennis courts laid end to end. A ship this big takes over 6km (4 miles) to stop at sea.

DID YOU KNOW?

The first successful submarine was built in the 1620's by a Dutch inventor, Cornelius van Drebbel. It had a wooden frame covered in greased leather and was rowed along with 12 oars. The biggest submarines today are Russian nuclear submarines. Larger than passenger liners, they can stay under for two years without refuelling.

Raft journey

In 1947 the explorer, Thor Heyerdahl, set out in his balsa-wood raft, *Kon-tiki,* to sail from Peru to the Pacific Islands. He wanted to prove that Inca people could have made this journey 1,500 years ago. The crew lived on fish and rainwater, as the Incas had done. Less than four months later they reached the Pacific island of Raroia.

Speed at sea

The speed of a ship is measured in knots. One knot is the speed of one nautical mile (1.85km or 1.15 land miles) per hour. In the past sailors trailed a knotted rope in the water to see how fast the ship was going. The knots were evenly spaced. By counting the number of knots let out over a set time of 28 seconds, a sailor could measure how fast the ship was going.

Some famous shipwrecks

Ship	Date sank	Cargo recovered
Kyrenia ship (Greece)	4th century BC	400 wine amphoras; 10,000 almonds
Mary Rose (England)	1545	Sundials; arrows; shoes; surgeon's knife
La Trinidad Valencera (Spain)	1588	Bronze cannons weighing 2.5 tonnes each
Wasa (Sweden)	1628	Sails; bronze guns; bodies with clothes on
Vergulde Draeck (Holland)	1656	8 chests of silver
HMS Edinburgh (Great Britain)	1942	5.5 tonnes of gold bars, worth £45 million

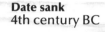

Amazing But True

In 1836 the wooden paddle-steamer, *Royal Tar,* was destroyed by fire and sank. Most of its unusual cargo was lost. The ship had been carrying a collection of snakes and birds, an elephant, two lions, a tiger, two camels, some horses and a group of circus performers, including a brass band.

Iceberg ahoy

Icebergs are a hidden danger to ships because only about one eighth of the ice shows above the water. The *Titanic* was one of the biggest ships ever built. On her first voyage in 1912 she hit an iceberg in the north Atlantic and sank 4,000m (13,000ft) under the sea. Over 1,500 of the ship's passengers died.

Finding the way

For many years sailors navigated by the Sun, Moon and stars. They used instruments called sextants to plot the ship's position by measuring the height of the Sun or Moon above the horizon at a certain time of day. Radio, radar and satellites have now made navigation much more accurate.

Ocean resources

Sea harvest

Each year some 70 to 75 million tonnes of fish are caught in the oceans. Over half comes from the Pacific. The largest single catch ever was made by a Norwegian boat in 1986. It contained over 120 million fish, enough for each Norwegian to have 30 fish each.

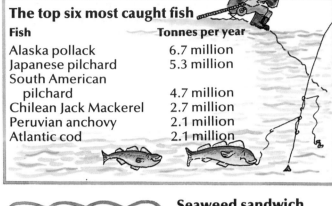

The top six most caught fish

Fish	Tonnes per year
Alaska pollack	6.7 million
Japanese pilchard	5.3 million
South American pilchard	4.7 million
Chilean Jack Mackerel	2.7 million
Peruvian anchovy	2.1 million
Atlantic cod	2.1 million

Fish farming

Many countries breed fish and shellfish in underwater farms. On fish farms, plaice grow to adult size in about 18-24 months, about half the time they would take in the wild. They are also easier to catch than in the open sea.

DID YOU KNOW?

About 6 million tonnes of salt are taken from the sea each year. This is enough to build a salt version of the Great Pyramid in Egypt. In hot countries, people use a very simple method to collect salt from the sea. Huge, shallow pans are arranged along the coast. These fill up with sea water as the tide comes in. The water dries up in the hot Sun, leaving the salt behind.

Seaweed sandwich

Seaweed is full of vitamins and calcium. In China and Japan huge amounts are harvested and eaten. In Ireland it is spread over the fields as fertilizer. Seaweed is also used to thicken ice cream and to make shampoo, toothpaste and even explosives.

Gold mine

Sea water contains about 100 times more gold than people own in the world. Sea gold has already been mined on the coasts of Alaska. If all the sea gold could be mined, there would be enough for each person on Earth to have a piece weighing 1kg (2.2lb).

Ocean oil

Over a fifth of the world's oil comes from the sea bed. Oil formed millions of years ago from the bodies of tiny sea animals and plants which drifted to the sea bed and were covered in layers of mud and sand. A single North Sea oil rig produces enough oil in one day to fill 70,000 cars with petrol.

Rich droppings

Cormorant droppings, or guano, are the world's most valuable natural fertilizer, about 30 times richer than farmyard manure. About 50 years ago, 5.5 million cormorants nested off the coasts of Peru. In places on the cliffs their guano was an amazing 164ft (50m) thick.

The top offshore crude oil producers (Thousands of barrels a day)	
UK	2,237
Mexico	1,700
USA	1,257
Saudi Arabia	1,107
Venezuela	900

Amazing But True

Some scientists think that Antarctic icebergs could provide desert areas with fresh water. Tugs could tow large icebergs across the Southern Ocean at a rate of 40km (25 miles) a day to Australia and Chile. The journey would take about four months but only half the ice would melt on the way.

Deep-sea nodules

A quarter of the sea floor deep under the Pacific is covered in millions of black, potato-sized lumps, or nodules. These contain valuable metals, such as manganese, iron, copper and nickel. Over millions of years the nodules grow in layers around grains of sand or sharks' teeth.

Taming the tides

Scientists are now looking to the sea as a source of energy. The world's first large tidal power station was built on the River Rance in France. A dam with 24 tunnels in it runs across the river mouth. As the tides rush in and out, they turn generators in the tunnels to produce electricity. Each generator makes enough power to light a medium-sized town.

Oceans in danger

Dirty water

Over 80 per cent of the waste which pollutes the oceans comes from the land. Here are some of the main causes of ocean pollution:

1 Sewage pumped straight into the sea.
2 Poisonous metals, such as mercury, tin and lead which come from factories, mines and boats.
3 Nuclear waste from power stations.
4 Chemical fertilizers and pesticides, washed off farmland and carried by rivers into the sea.
5 Oil and petrol are washed off the land into the sea. Oil also comes from oil tanker accidents and oil rigs.

Suffocated sea

In summer, parts of the Adriatic Sea are covered in a thick, green slime of plant plankton. The plankton uses sewage and fertilizers washed into the sea to grow. It blocks out sunlight which other sea plants need to make food. As it decays, it uses so much oxygen that fish and shellfish suffocate.

Oil slick

In March 1989 the huge oil tanker, *Exxon Valdez*, ran aground in Prince William Sound, Alaska. The ship poured some 45 million litres of oil into the sea in one of the worst oil spills ever known. Some 100,000 sea birds died as their feathers became clogged with oil and lost their warmth. They included 150 rare bald eagles. About 1,000 sea otters and hundreds of thousands of fish, seals and shellfish also died.

Overfishing

As the number of people in the world grows, so does the need for more food. Fish are being taken from the sea faster than they can grow and restock. In 1965 about 250,000 haddock were caught in the North Atlantic. By 1974 this had dropped to 20,000. Some countries now have limits on how many fish can be caught each year. Others use nets with a large mesh to let young fish escape.

Amazing But True

Each year thousands of sea birds and mammals die when they become entangled in drift nets, used for catching squid. These plastic nets are trailed across the ocean like giant walls. Each net may be 20km (12 miles) long. Over 48,000km (30,000 miles) of net may be used by just one fleet of boats.

Rubbish tip

The oceans are the biggest rubbish tip on Earth. Ships dump about 6 million tonnes of rubbish into the sea every year. It includes glass bottles, tins, plastic containers, wire, wood and food.

Marine park

The Great Barrier Reef is home to 400 species of coral and 1,500 species of fish. But coral reefs all over the world are in danger from tourists, pollution and overfishing. In 1980 the Barrier Reef Marine Park was set up to protect the reef. There are now special areas set aside for nesting sites, research zones, fishing zones and for tourists.

Keep Out

Sea animals in danger

Blue whale		Originally some 250,000 in the Southern Ocean. Today as few as 11,000 are left.
Fin whale		Numbers have dropped from 500,000 to 120,000.
Kemps Ridley turtle		Once common in the Gulf of Mexico but killed for meat, shells and eggs.
Florida manatee		Killed for meat. Fewer than 1,000 are left.
Juan Fernandez fur seal		One of the rarest seals. Only about 705 are left.
Sea otter		Hunted for fur. Now protected and numbers have risen steadily.

DID YOU KNOW?

Many sea animals have already died out (become extinct). The great auk used to live in the North Atlantic Ocean. It could not fly and was easy to catch for its fat, meat and feathers. People were also afraid of it. In 1834 a great auk was killed in Ireland because it was thought to be a witch. The last great auk ever was killed in 1844.

Fight for survival

The Mediterranean monk seal is Europe's most endangered mammal. So many seals have been killed for their meat and skins and by fishermen who consider them a pest that there are fewer than 500 now left.

Law of the Sea

The Law of the Sea aims to protect the sea and control how it is used. It was drawn up by the United Nations in 1982. It divides the sea up into areas for different countries leaving about two thirds of the open ocean free for all.

Sea myths and legends

Abandoned ship

On 3 December 1872, a ship called the *Marie Celeste* was found drifting in the Atlantic Ocean. The whole crew had completely vanished, leaving their breakfasts half eaten on the table. No clues to the crew's whereabouts have ever been found.

Sunk without trace

The legendary island of Atlantis flourished in about 10,000 BC. Then the island was destroyed by a volcanic eruption and sank without trace. No one really knows if Atlantis ever existed but there are many suggestions of where it might have been. These include the Greek island, Santorini and the Canary Islands.

Amazing But True

The Bermuda Triangle is a large stretch of the Atlantic Ocean between Bermuda, Miami and Puerto Rico. Many ships and even aircraft have disappeared here without trace. Some people believe that the vanishing ships and aircraft are hijacked by UFOs and their crews kidnapped by aliens.

Ghost ship

The *Flying Dutchman* is said to bring bad luck to anyone who sees her. The ship left Amsterdam for the East Indies in the 17th century. On the way she was hit by fierce winds but the captain refused to change course. A ghostly devil dared the captain to sail straight into the storm. The captain did so and the ship was doomed to haunt the seas for ever.

Sea monsters

There have been hundreds of reports of terrifying sea monsters. Norse legends tell of the huge "kraken" which could easily overturn a ship. The kraken was a cross between a squid and an octopus. It had suckers and claws, and a beaky mouth strong enough to bore through a ship. The legend is probably based on the giant squid.

Sea dragons

In Chinese mythology, the seas were ruled over by four great dragon kings. Each lived in a crystal palace and commanded a huge army. The army included fish, crayfish, crabs and watchmen who patrolled the bottom of the sea.

Finger seals

Sedna is the Eskimo goddess of the sea. She was taken from home by a sea bird disguised as a handsome man. Her father rescued her but a fierce storm hit their boat. To calm the storm gods, her father threw Sedna into the sea. As she gripped the boat, he cut off her fingers which turned into seals, whales and walruses.

Gift of the tides

A Japanese legend tells how the sea god gave the tides to another god, Hikohohodemi, as a gift. Hikohohodemi went to the bottom of the sea to find a lost fish hook. While he was there, the sea god gave him two jewels. One made the tide rise and the other made it fall. By throwing the jewels in the sea, Hikohohodemi could control the water.

Ocean gods

For thousands of years, people who rely on the sea for their living and safety have worshipped sea gods and goddesses.

People	Sea god
Ancient Greeks	Poseidon
Romans	Neptune
Ancient Egyptians	Nun
Chinese	T'ien Hou (the goddess of sailors)
Japanese	O-Wata-Tsu-Mi
Tahitians	Ruahatu
Eskimos	Sedna
Celts	Manannan

DID YOU KNOW?

A Polynesian legend tells how the world was created in a giant clam. At first there was only a sea and a goddess, Old Spider. She picked up a giant clam and squeezed inside it. There she found two snails and a worm. She made the smaller snail the Moon and the larger snail the Sun. Half the clam shell became the Earth, the other half the sky and the worm's salty sweat the sea.

Dolphin rescue

A Greek legend tells how dolpins saved the life of the musician, Arion. He was sailing back to Greece after winning a music competition in Italy. The ship's crew wanted the prizes he had won and attacked him. They allowed him to play one last tune which attracted a school of dolphins to the ship. Arion quickly leapt overboard and was carried safely home on a dolphin's back.

Ocean record breakers

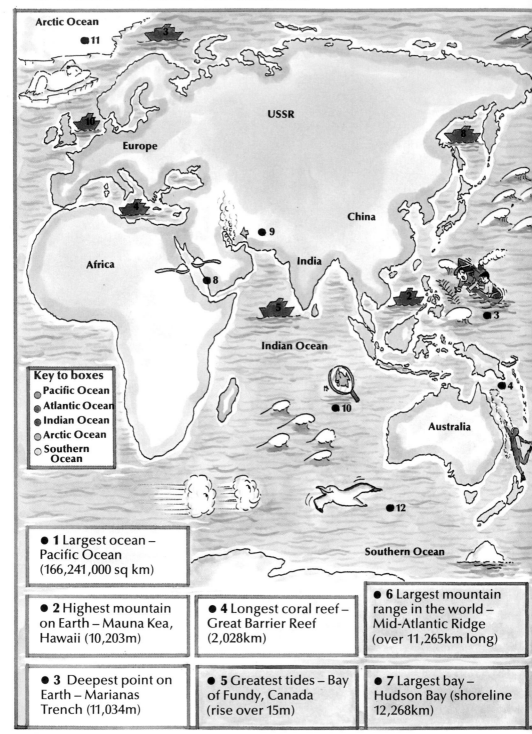

Arctic Ocean

USSR

Europe

China

Africa

India

Indian Ocean

Australia

Southern Ocean

Key to boxes
- Pacific Ocean
- Atlantic Ocean
- Indian Ocean
- Arctic Ocean
- Southern Ocean

● **1** Largest ocean – Pacific Ocean (166,241,000 sq km)

● **2** Highest mountain on Earth – Mauna Kea, Hawaii (10,203m)

● **3** Deepest point on Earth – Marianas Trench (11,034m)

● **4** Longest coral reef – Great Barrier Reef (2,028km)

● **5** Greatest tides – Bay of Fundy, Canada (rise over 15m)

● **6** Largest mountain range in the world – Mid-Atlantic Ridge (over 11,265km long)

● **7** Largest bay – Hudson Bay (shoreline 12,268km)

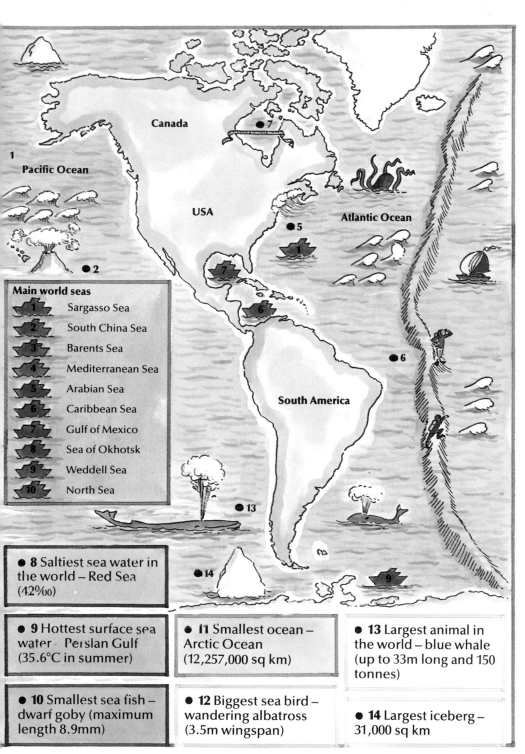

Canada

Pacific Ocean

1

USA

Atlantic Ocean

● 2

Main world seas

1	Sargasso Sea	
2	South China Sea	
3	Barents Sea	
4	Mediterranean Sea	
5	Arabian Sea	
6	Caribbean Sea	
7	Gulf of Mexico	
8	Sea of Okhotsk	
9	Weddell Sea	
10	North Sea	

● 5

● 7

● 6

South America

● 6

● 13

● 14

● 9

● **8** Saltiest sea water in
the world – Red Sea
(42‰)

● **9** Hottest surface sea
water – Persian Gulf
(35.6°C in summer)

● **10** Smallest sea fish –
dwarf goby (maximum
length 8.9mm)

● **11** Smallest ocean –
Arctic Ocean
(12,257,000 sq km)

● **12** Biggest sea bird –
wandering albatross
(3.5m wingspan)

● **13** Largest animal in
the world – blue whale
(up to 33m long and 150
tonnes)

● **14** Largest iceberg –
31,000 sq km

Glossary

Abyssal plain A vast, flat area of the ocean floor, below 4km (2.5 miles).

Algae A group of simple plants ranging from tiny one-celled plants to giant seaweeds.

Atoll A horseshoe-shaped or circular coral island around a deep lagoon.

Continental shelf The shallow sea bed around the continents, not deeper than 200m (656ft) below sea level.

Continental slope The sloping area leading from the continental shelf to the abyssal plain.

Crustaceans A group of sea animals with hard shells. Lobsters, crabs and shrimps are all types of crustaceans.

Current A huge river of water running through the sea.

Dinoflagellates Tiny one-celled sea plants. Some are poisonous; others can produce their own light.

Invertebrate An animal without a backbone.

Knot A measurement of speed at sea. One knot equals 1.85kph (1.15mph).

Mammal A warm-blooded animal with a backbone. Mammals feed their young on milk.

Molluscs A large invertebrate group, often with shells. They range from giant squid to limpets and scallops.

Oceanography The scientific study of the oceans and seas.

Ooze A fine, smooth mud covering the sea floor. Made of the bodies of countless sea plants and animals.

Phytoplankton Tiny sea plants.

Pinnipedes A group of sea mammals which includes seals, sea-lions and walruses.

Plankton Tiny plants and animals which drift on the surface of the sea.

Plate A piece of the Earth's hard crust.

Polyp A tiny sea animal about 5mm (0.2in) long. Coral is made up of the hard skeletons of millions of polyps.

Salinity The saltiness of sea water.

Seamount An underwater volcano which never grows above sea level.

Seaquake An underwater earthquake.

Sediment Pieces of mud, sand and rock which settle on the sea bed.

Siphonophore A sea animal, such as a Portuguese man-of-war, which is made up of a colony of tiny animals.

Spreading ridge An underwater mountain range, formed when liquid rock rises to fill cracks in the sea floor.

Subduction zone The place where two underwater plates collide. One plate is pushed underneath the other.

Submersible A free-moving submarine vehicle for carrying ocean scientists.

Trench A deep, V-shaped dip in the sea floor, formed at a subduction zone.

Turbidity current An avalanche of mud and sand which may be caused by an earthquake.

Water pressure The weight of water pressing down on things in the sea.

Index